IN LOVE WITH THE KING OF COMPTON

QUEEN KEISHII

Published by Urban Chapters Publications

www.urbanchapterspublications.com

Contains explicit languages and adult themes

suitable for ages 16+

ACKNOWLEDGMENTS

First and foremost, I have to give all of my thanks to God and I know that without Him, NOTHING in my life would be possible. Tell God your plans and watch Him laugh.

In the same way, let your light shine before others, that they may see your good deeds and glorify your Father in Heaven.

-Matthew 5:14 NIV

I would like to give a special thanks to my mother and sister for being there for me and giving me advice when I needed.

I would like to thank my beautiful publisher, Jahquel J. for extending the invite to be a part of a great company. She made it possible for me to follow my dreams and I'm glad to be a part of Urban Chapters Publications. She gonna have to drag me out because it's #UCP forever, if you didn't know. This lady is soooo damn talented and it's a pleasure that she took me under her wing.

I wanna take the time out to thank Treasure Malian. You have given me some great advice and helped me build my brand so much in the last year. I want you to know that it is appreciated lady.

I would like to thank all of the authors out there that have motivated me and continue to work on their craft. We are all talented, so don't forget it.

I also want to thank my best friends and my fiancé for being there through it all. I'm not going to write a big paragraph, but y'all know what it is.

Last, but not least, I would like to thank the readers for continuing to be there for me and ride this Queen Keishii wave. I promise you that I do it for y'all. I want you all to see my growth whenever you pick up a book of mine.

ABOUT THE AUTHOR

Contact Me
Website: www.keishturner.com
Facebook: Keish Andrea / Queen Keishii
IG: @_keys2bequeened
Snapchat: @respect_keishii
Twitter: @GottaLuv_Keish

Letter From The Author,

Book #17 ! I'm surprised that I was able to finish another one. After two years in this writing game, I still am humbled when I release a book. This book here— chilllleee! It tested me like I was an extra on Lean On Me! (chuckles) I want to thank you all for your continued support of me and I love you all. All of the inboxes, comments, and tags do not go unnoticed and I deeply appreciate them all. I love my day one readers and all the new readers all the same. All of y'all are dope. Every process of writing a book is different. This book took me through some emotion mannnnn! It was crazy how I got lost in some of these characters. I coddled this one for way too long to try and make it perfect. I try to provide a story that all of you can get lost in. I hope I accomplished that with this new one. I tried my best to embody Compton in this book. Please don't chew me out is some things are off. Look forward to hearing from you guys about how you like or dislike the book.

Thank you for the lasting support.

-Keish

1

HEAVY

*H*eavy stood in the dank, old basement of the trap house, with a deep grimace on his face. There were several men on the side of him, watching and anticipating what he was about to do to Doon. Doon sat on the floor, shaking like a leaf in the wind. He was scared and sure that everyone could smell the fear seeping from his pores.

"*AGGGGGGGHHHHH!*" This treacherous nigga had the nerve to scream as Heavy severed his wrist and foot from his body. The machete making contact with his skin made a swoosh sound.

SWOOSH!

This nigga, Doon thought he was going to steal from Heavy and then run his mouth when the cops caught up with his dumb ass. Heavy knew for a fact that he snitched on him, too. That's what fuck-boys do when their backs are against the wall. The affidavit littered out of the folder, right on the side of him. This nigga was singing more than Anita Baker when she hit them fucking high notes in her songs. Thought my boy was solid and turns out he was a straight bitch! Heavy spoke inwardly to himself, pissed off.

"Doon, why the fuck yo' hoe ass out here snitching, homie?" Heavy was still holding the machete in his hand, waiting for him to lie.

The main things he hated in this world were snitches, liars, body odor, and begging ass people. Those were his pet peeves and could earn yo' ass a bullet to the skull. Doon was going to learn what it meant to cross the BHM and Heavy.

"They. Told. Me. That. They. Had. All. This. Evidence. Against. Me. And. I. Would. Go. Away. For. Life," this was the dumb ass response that homie gave Heavy.

Gallardo looked at everyone else in the room to see if he heard him clearly. His right hand, Zip looked at him and started bursting out laughing. *Clown ass nigga,* Heavy mouthed. Zip's ass could never be serious. He was a goofy ass nigga, but he handled his business. Yo' ass should be very afraid if he wasn't laughing. That was rare, but it meant that ya would feel his wrath.

"What the fuck does that matter to me? Doon, you was caught with the shit you stole from me. How you turn around and sell out the only nigga that has helped you? That's what the fuck I'm curious to know. I gave you work when yo' ugly ass granny was doing bad and needed that surgery and this is how you repay me— okay," Heavy was enraged as he talked to Doon.

"Heavy. Have. Mercy. On. Me. Please." Doon begged in between his panting.

He had Heavy fucked up if he would let him be after this nigga was willing to turn state evidence on him. No nigga would catch him slipping like they did his dad and uncle. He didn't give a fuck who it was.

"Mercy? Nigga, you didn't hesitate to talk to the cops like I wouldn't figure it out. When you get to hell, tell them Heavy sends his regards. I'm sure the Devil got a throne waiting on me."

Heavy took the machete and decapitated his ass. His head fell clean off of his body with a loud thud. He was in a zone and didn't give a damn if anyone in the room was squeamish or scared. Pussy shit wasn't tolerated in this crew, so it was best to get rid of the weak niggas now or forever taint ya squad. There was no room for snitches in Heavy's world. Doon had to learn the hard way. *I hope this showed the rest of these niggas that I wasn't playing out here in these streets,*

Heavy thought, his temper still in full force. The Black Mask Militia was here to stay and they were as strong as their weakest link. Heavy would work overtime to kill off anybody that he had to.

"This go for any of you niggas that feel like they are going to go against the grain. It don't matter who you are, I will kill ya ass. This nigga head went bloopity bloop on the floor with no hesitation. Let Doon be yo' lesson not to cross this Militia. It's in yo' best interest not to." Zip warned, as he lit the joint in his mouth.

"Get this shit cleaned up. Mail his pieces to his babymama and brother. Send his granny twenty grand. I always liked her and she isn't to blame for having a fucked up nephew. Meeting is adjourned!" Heavy threw the machete down to the cold, steel ground and removed his shirt and the sweats he was wearing.

They were covered in specks of that nigga's blood. He washed my hands in the faucet that was built near the door. Heavy lathered them with soap and made sure he got in the nail beds and his wrists. Heavy was big on cleanliness, so he made sure all parts of his body were thoroughly washed at all times. That was also the quickest way to get a case built on you, especially if one time pulled you over. They would use all of that circumstantial evidence to have you seeing football numbers in the pen. Heavy wasn't on that type of time.

He had on some baller shorts and a wife beater underneath the bloody clothes. Heavy walked out of the trap house and jumped in his matte black Mercedes-Benz G-Wagon. He was tired as shit and just wanted to take a little nap before he headed back into the streets.

Heavy hadn't been sleep in over thirty hours. The chorus to Kanye West's song 30 Hours was ringing in his head. His body was craving his Tempur Pedic California King bed. Heavy's bones ached from all the running around he had been doing. Heavy lived in a pretty decent three bedroom, two bath house on W. Johnston Street in Compton, California.

They called it "*Bompton*" though because they were blood gang affiliated. Heavy's dad and uncle were Blood gang through and through. He took over their businesses, but decided not to fully become a Blood. There was too much shit that came with that life.

His dad and uncle were both sitting in the maximum security prison, *San Quentin* for life without parole. The *RICO* laws and all of that other shit that gang life brought you was responsible for that. They had their hand in the drug game, rap game, counterfeiting of goods and the prostitution game. Heavy didn't like the idea of running hoes and selling knockoffs, so that was not a part of his organization. He had sisters and respected women too much and loved fashion too much to do something like that. He also promised his mother to leave that part of the life alone. They had their hands in diamond broker-ing, real estate, drug distribution, and the stealing of foreign cars. Heavy ran the organization like a *Fortune 500* company. He felt like that was better than any other way that criminal enterprises were ran. People didn't get that until they were downtown at a federal court appearance or slumped somewhere in an alley. Those were not options for him. Heavy was too smart to be trapped in bullshit.

His name was Gallardo (that's his real name) Miller and he was the only son of Gene and Serita Miller. His parents gave birth to two other girls, his sisters, Gretchen and Gina. They were nineteen and twenty-two. Heavy was the oldest at twenty-four. His parents were still married til this day and his mama held his pops down. He's been locked up for six years now. Heavy's been running things since he was eighteen. His uncle, Trip was right in there with him. They left every-thing to himself and his cousin, Zacarion aka Zip. Yep. The goofy ass nigga is Heavy's right hand and his cousin. They've been joined at the hip since they came out the cooch. He couldn't run this organization without him.

€€€€€€€

He pulled up to my crib and let out a delightful sigh. Driving these LA streets had him about to fall asleep behind the wheel, but he made it home. He said a quick prayer up to the most high and then got out of my car. Heavy armed the alarm and headed to the front door to open it. As he opened the door, he smelled something good cooking. He surmised that as only being my mama or one of my little sisters in the kitchen cooking. He didn't give women the keys to his crib and jump-offs weren't allowed to enter. He wasn't with that *A Thin Line Between Love and Hate* type of stuff going on. Heavy eliminated the possibility of it being his mama, when he heard YG's *Bool, Balm, and Bollected* blaring through the speakers. That song was raw. Heavy didn't know the homie, but they did run in the same circle. He walked into the kitchen and saw his sister, Gretchen dancing as she cooked in the kitchen. His little sister spotted him and turned the volume of the music down.

"Big brother! Heyyyyy!" She jumped into his arms like she always did.

He enjoyed the bond that him and his little sisters had. They worked his nerves, but they were close-knit in my family.

"Wassup, GG," Heavy called her by her nickname.

"Needed a little break from the dorms at *UCLA*, so I decided to come stay with you for a few days. That's cool? I'm not going to catch some hoes running up and down the house, am I ?"

"Naw, sis. I don't bring females to the crib. That ain't even the move." He scrunched his face up as she hopped down from in my arms.

"I had to check. I stayed with Zip's crazy ass last night and he had some chick running out of his house, in only her panties. I asked him why she was running and he told me that he couldn't fuck with her because her pussy was rotten." Gretchen and Heavy shared a laugh.

"What are you cooking?" He tried to look in the pot, but that earned him a smack to the hands.

"Don't touch my pots, fool! I'm cooking baked chicken, macaroni and cheese, and southwestern green beans."

"Damn, that sound good as hell! Make sure you let me know when it's done. I'm about to hop in the shower and crash." Heavy grabbed a Gatorade and a Fiji water from the fridge and went to my room.

Once he reached the room, he closed my door behind him. Heavy placed the bottles on my nightstand and kicked his shoes off. He pulled the wife beater off and laid across the bed. He was so tired that he couldn't move for a second.

As he dozed off, his personal cellphone chimed to let me know he had a message. He picked it up from the bed and it was from this chick named, Mia. She was from Baldwin Hills and he met her in the mall. Baby was caramel and thick. Heavy licked his lips as he imagined the things that she did to him during their last sexual encounter. He felt his man below stiffening, in anticipation of the creaminess ahead.

Mia: You gonna be at yo' club tonight?
Heavy: I may swing through for a lil bit. Why?
Mia: You trying to have me before the club.

Heavy: Aight

Heavy threw his phone back on the bed and succumbed to some much needed sleep.

€€€€€€€

It must have been hours later because the sun was going down, when Heavy opened his eyes. He decided to jump into the shower. He walked into the bathroom and stripped out of my clothes. Heavy turned on the shower with the jets coming out of the sides and the rainforest shower head. All of this was doing wonders for his body. The aches were slowly disappearing. He lathered his body with his Bvlgari Man body wash and took care of his other hygienic needs.

He changed into a pair of black cut off Levi's and a throwback black and white Los Angeles Dodgers baseball jersey. He had to stop by and tighten Mia up before went out to the club. He threw on a Black Mask Militia hat. To finish off his attire, he threw on a pair of all white Yeezy Boost 360s.

When he walked out of the room, he heard Gretchen talking to someone. That made his blood boil because his lil sis knew he didn't like company. Nobody but his sisters, his mother, and his niggas knew where he lived at. Gallardo made sure of that, so a nigga wouldn't think about ever trying to catch him slipping. He was just about to check her lil ass, until I saw who it was. This girl was beautiful as shit to Heavy. She was short in stature maybe like 5'3 or 5'4, the color of lightly toasted coconut, her hair was curly and wild, and she had these lips that he wouldn't mind kissing all day long. Baby girl was bad, even in the Adidas leggings and UCLA Bruins tee she was wearing. She also had these glasses on her face that made her look like a sexy ass geek. Her eyes had him hooked, he didn't know what color they were but they were pretty.

"Ay, sis, I'm about to be out. You got a key in case I'm back late."

"Big bruh, come here." Gretchen gestured for him to come to her. He obliged her and walked over.

"Before you can be rude, I'm going to introduce y'all. Gallardo, this is my bestie, Nikayla. Nik Nik, this is my brother, Gallardo."

"Nice to meet you, ma." He shook her hand into his.

"Nice to meet you as well." Nikayla responded, in that sexy, silky little voice of hers.

"Well, y'all be easy. I'm about to be out," He closed the door behind him and jumped back in the truck.

It was only going to take him fifteen minutes to get to Carson from where he stayed. Heavy stopped at the *Rite Aid,* a few blocks from the crib. He jumped out of the G-Wagon and walked right to the aisle where the condoms were. He grabbed a three pack of Magnum Ecstasy condoms and some Axe body wash. He refused to walk around smelling like Mia and that fruity and floral shit she wore. Heavy grabbed a tropical bag of Skittles as he stood in line. Due to his jersey being open, his tattoos on his chest and neck were on full display. It was hot as hell in LA, so it was a necessity to keep it open. There were several women in the store that were looking at him with lust in their eyes. They were kind of out of luck because all he was focused on was sliding in Mia's pussy and letting her give him head. He had flavored condoms for that because she had good pussy, but he ain't trust these bitches. He made his purchases and got back on the road.

As he was almost a block away from the hotel, his phone rang and it sounded off through the Bluetooth system. Heavy answered it and it was his cousin, Zip's goofy ass.

"Ay, wassup, pretty ass nigga." He was choking as he was laughing and Heavy automatically knew he was getting high.

"Yeah, whatever. What you up to besides smoking bud?"

"About to get some grub before I head to the club tonight. You coming through?" He took another pull of the dank he was smoking.

"I might swing through after I finish fucking with Mia. She called me from the telly in Carson."

"Aight, well, hit me up when you done with that. I'm about to pull up in this drive-thru."

"Aight, Keep them eyes open because them niggas plotting. Have the banga on ya to show em the militia behind ya." Heavy recited their creed to his cousin.

It was their way of telling each other to be careful because dudes would love to murk a militia nigga.

"Same shit, different day, when the Militia behind ya." Zip responded, in comprehension of what he was saying.

They talked for a few more seconds and then hung up. Heavy arrived at the Double Tree and killed the engine. He had to text Mia to ask her what room it was.

Heavy: Aight, I'll be up in a few.

Heavy took the elevator to the sixth floor and walked to the room. He knocked on the door and Mia opened it. She was naked as the day she was born and his dick instantly rose up, in appreciation.

"Thank you for coming." Mia spoke, in a sultry voice.

"That's no problem, sexy. So, what you want first? You want me to beat them walls up or you wanna swallow this dick?" He arched my eyebrows, in curiosity.

"I want you to feel what this mouth can do. Pass me a condom, Heavy." Mia looked up at him with the captivating light brown eyes of hers.

She called him by his street name like everyone else who wasn't family or a close friend. He tried to keep people from knowing my government, it kept down the snitching level. Gallardo is a gangster ass name, but he didn't want everyone calling me something that my mama and sisters called him.

Heavy passed Mia the condom and she proceeded to suck the skin off of his shit like she always did. Heavy kept her around for that reason, mostly. She had to have been fucking someone else with deep pockets because she drove an Aston Martin Vanquish, stayed fresh in designer shit, and kept her appearance up. He didn't ball out on her, so it definitely didn't come from him. He didn't care where it was coming from. Their relationship was basically driven by sex, nothing more, nothing less. Heavy leaned his head back and enjoyed the sensations of her jaws sucking him in. If Mia didn't know how to do anything else, she knew how to suck some dick.

€€€€€€€

Later that night...

Heavy was sitting in his custom VIP section inside of his night-club, Noir. He nodding his head to Young Jeezy's *All There*. Jeezy was Heavy's favorite Southern rapper because his music banged. Heavy sat in the section with his Dopeboy 95 Air Maxes on, just like the song said. He changed into a black short-sleeved button up, black Levi's, and all black Nike Air Max 95s. He had an all black LA Dodgers hat covering his eyes. The only jewelry he had on was a gold Rolex and a Cuban link around his neck. Zip, Tress, KB, and Burnah sat in the section with him. They were the main niggas in the *Black Mask Militia*. Nothing moved without them knowing. You rarely saw them out, so when you did, they made sure that it was a movie. This night would be no different.

"We need eight bottles of White Hennessy and three bottles of Ace of Spades sent to the section," Zip directed to the bottle girl, Ming Si.

Ming Si was this bad ass Blaisian (Black/ Asian) chick that was the head bottle girl. Heavy slid in them guts once, but she couldn't handle the dick. She had all of that ass for nothing if you asked him. Last he heard, she let some of the Black Mask Militia niggas hit. Heavy couldn't be mad because she wasn't his girl. The fact that she fucked with dudes that were runners and lookouts, let him know that Ming Si could never be on the same level playing field as him. She was expendable just like every one of these girls that came his way. He was not the settling down type.

"Ay, Ming Si, you trying to leave with me tonight?" KB looked up from his phone and questioned her.

She looked over at Heavy and he shrugged his shoulders, nonchalantly. I mean...what did she want me to say? If you trying to let the homie beat them guts in, then by all means, let that shit rock. Heavy thought, trying his best not to laugh.

"Bye, KB. I'll bring y'all bottles back," she rolled her eyes and walked from the section with plenty of attitude.

All of them started bursting out laughing because they knew that KB was trying to test her. Ming Si didn't know that the crew had her on that list for a pass around. The pussy was garbage, but she had a good head on her shoulders. Just thinking about that awesome jawsome, had Heavy's dick slowly rising. He coughed and the heat died down in his body.

"KB, you a wild ass dude!" Zip laughed out loud, with his goofy ass.

"That bitch really think she not a pass around or a straight bop. She bad as fuck, I'll tell you that." KB quipped, taking a puff of the joint he was smoking.

As they continued to laugh and joke, Heavy's little sisters, Gretchen and Gina and their friend, Nikayah walked up to the section. Heavy couldn't keep his eyes off of Nikayla and he was sure that she felt him staring, even though she couldn't see his eyes. She was wearing the hell out of this white dress. It curved on her body like a glove. Clearly shorty was one of the baddest in the club. She had her wild hair up in some kind of bun at the top of her head. Her beautiful caramel legs were on display and the heels she had on, made him picture her legs sitting on his shoulders as he hit her on the counter in my kitchen.

"Oh shit, I think this is the first time that this nigga has ever been speechless," Zip jested, making everyone in the section laugh their ass off.

2

NIKAYLA

*N*ikayla wasn't sure when they decided to go out, but they were headed to this club called *Noir*. Gretchen explained that the club was owned by her sexy ass brother, Gallardo. That nigga was too fine for his own good. Nikayla made a vow to not mess with any more thugs, but he could get it. That 6'3, milk chocolate Adonis had her lady parts reacting in the worst way. His eyes would make any woman swoon. They were a beautiful shade of brown with gold flecks in them. Just pure sexiness, all wrapped in one package. It had been two years since Nikayla had any type of sexual contact.

The last two years of her life have been crazy. Her baby, Nahem's father, Nathan was killed after he led the police on a high-speed chase. He was out robbing banks to help support us. Nikayla didn't know until she saw the harrowing details unfolding on the nightly news. She couldn't believe that he went out like that. Now, Nikayla was here raising their seven-year-old son, alone. The pain she felt from Nathan's death was finally bearable and she felt like it was time to move on. Nikayla didn't think that Gallardo would be that person, seeing as though he was the head of the *Black Mask Militia*. They were ruthless and connected to most of the crime happening in LA, hell, from California to wherever else their reach went. He was this big kingpin and she didn't need that type of attention in her life.

She was a simple girl just raising a young king in this world. Before we continue, Nikayah Anderson was a twenty-two-year-old RN at the *University of Central Los Angeles Medical Center*. She really loved her job. Nikayla took pride in her job, her son, and school. She attended *UCLA*, obtaining her Masters in nursing. She was in school to be a nurse practitioner by the time she was twenty-five. Nikayla was almost there by the grace of God and her ambition. Nothing was going to deter her from her dreams. She felt like thug niggas and the life that they lived had the power to come through and mess all of that up. Also, she was striving to prove that just because she had her son at fifteen, she still was out here grinding so that he could have a wonderful life.

"Sis, turn on Mila J, while we pregame," Gretchen stated to Nikayla, as she applied on her makeup.

Nikayla felt like her best friend was bad with or without makeup. She could be a makeup artist if she wanted, but Gretchen was interested in being an architect. That was her dream and she was good at it. Both of them had a head on their shoulders. They were staying on campus in a dorm-like apartment to save up for a house. GG could easily go to her brother, but that's not how she operated. She worked for everything she had and barely accepted money from Gallardo. Her little sister, Gina hung out with them when she was home from *Grambling State University*. She got a scholarship to play softball out there. She was only twenty, while they were a little older.

Nikayla turned it on Mila J's *"My Main."* It happened to be one of their favorite songs because it describes GG and Nikayla's friendship to a tee. The song was actually their unofficial anthem.

€€€€€€€

Once they were all ready, Nikayla and her girls looked like some snacks out here. Sweet enough to invade any nigga's wet dream. Nikayla wore this white Hermes lower thigh length, bodycon dress and a pair of gold Giuseppe Zanotti six-inch heels. They were a gift from Nathan before his death. Nikayla couldn't afford such an opulent pair of shoes on her own salary. Her legs would be on fire by the end of the night, but it was so worth it. She had a light beat to my face, courtesy of GG. Her best friend was slaying in a burnt orange Balenciaga bodycon dress and a pair of burnt orange, green, and black jungle Giuseppe Zanotti strap-up heels. They were so fucking beautiful and she knew that she was about to have bitches gassed and hating on them. That was why she was wearing them. They lived to stir pots and leave chicks in their feelings. They automatically labeled Nikayla and GG stuck up when they saw them. Too bad that's not who they were at all. Nikayla and GG were some of the most nice and down to earth women that you've ever met.

"I'm ready," Gina stood in the doorway as Nikayla placed the finished touches on her hair. The bun she was sporting took a little minute to perfect.

Gina was wearing this black romper that left little to the imagination. It looked so nice on her and she set it off with gold accessories and some spiked Christian Louboutin stilettos.

"Okay, we about to head out. Gina grab that José Cuervo and Parrot Bay from the freezer."

"Okay." Gina went to the kitchen to grab their pregame alcohol.

"Come take a pic with me sis," Nikayla told GG, as she stood and admired herself in the mirror.

GG walked over and joined her for their ghetto photo shoot on SnapChat and Instagram. They also went live on Instagram.

"Me and sis about to head out and paint the city platinum. The twerk twins are back and in full effect! We triplets tonight bih. Here go my sis, Gina. Baby is a baddie!" Gina came into the view of the camera twerking with her tongue hanging out.

"Get it bihhhhh," GG and Nikayla cheered her on.

They were all on *Snapchat* and *Instagram* acting a fool. Taking the party to the living room, they took the shots and drinks Gina prepared for their pregame. Nikayla was already feeling good, but she needed this turn up because these past few weeks have been trying for her. She just wanted to spend this night to unwind with her girls.

"So, y'all ready to walk up in here like we own the place?" Gretchen asked, as we sat at a red light.

"Yes ma'am. Shutting shit down as always."

"I'm trying to see Burnah. He is so fine to me." Gina gushed, with a deep smile on her face.

"Munchie, why you won't tell him that you like him?" Gretchen asked her little sister.

"I don't want Gallardo to feel some type of way that I am trying to talk to someone in his crew. Burnah run through bitches like I run through thongs." Gina responded, feeling like it would be doomed from the start.

"Well, shit, Gallardo just going to have to be mad. As far as him being a hoe, all niggas go through that hoe phase, but you're my sister, so I know that you can turn him out and make him be loyal to you. Y'all I want Tress big ass to pick me up and get it in. That nigga is too damn fine." GG gushed, playfully fanning herself.

"Bitch, I knew it! I knew you liked him. When was you going to tell me?" Nikayla fake pouted in her seat.

"Now, come on. I said I had a crush." Gretchen tried to smooth things over.

"Yeah, whatever. Let me find out that it's more than that and we boxing, trick." Nikayla threatened, playfully balling her fist up.

"Just like how you got a crush on Gallardo." Gretchen responded, smartly.

"Yo' brother is good looking, but no more thugs for me. I'm not trying to be with anyone. I'm only focused Naheem and finishing school." Niakayla tried to reiterate to her.

It would be cool to be with someone, but right now she felt like it would only be a distraction. That was not a distraction that she needed. She could not be knocked off of her square. Men have proven to be the downfall of a woman's ambition. Nikayla was not trying to be a statistic and join the ranks of the many dumb women that fell for some game and good dick.

€€€€€€€

Once arriving at *Noir*, they all were feeling pretty lit and lifted. Soon as GG parked her Audi, they all hopped out and headed straight to the front of the line. As usual, they heard the collective sighs, exaggerated huffs, and teeth sucks. They paid it no mind and made their way to the red velvet rope that separated them between the entrance and the bouncers.

"Hey, Big Loc." GG spoke sweetly to the big, strong man standing at the door.

Usually bouncers that stood out front of club were ugly as hell and perverted, but he was fine. He was the color of caramel filling in candy, had a low cut with his waves on swim, and he was built like he should be on a football field. He was wearing an all-black suit and dress shoes. He also had on this gold chain that looked like it could easily be a dog collar if it was smaller. Nikayla found this to be comical. She suppressed the urge to laugh. She knew he probably wouldn't let her in if she crowned him.

"Wassup, GG and Munchie." He spoke to Gretchen and Gina.

"Nothing much, boo. She's with us." Gretchen pointed to Nikayla and Loc allowed her entrance into the club. They walked into the club and it was packed as hell. It seemed like there was people from wall to wall. The club was almost dark, but had black and gold decor. There were three floors: the main floor, VIP, and then the office and rooftop restaurant. The place was so beautiful that Nikayla had to give Gallardo his props. Things were put together immaculately and rather impressive.

Lathun's *Freak It* was playing as they walked through the crowd, headed to the VIP sections. GG, Gina, and Nikayla danced where they stood and people made room. They started doing the line dance to the song. They were getting it in and the crowd was eating it up. Whenever the three of them linked up, it was always a party. When the ladies arrived in VIP, Nikayla could feel that Gallardo was staring at her. He seemed to be speechless or awestruck. *This man is so goddamn fine!* Nikayla mused to herself, feeling a familiar throbbing in her pussy. Made her have visions of riding him reverse- cowgirl on the very couch he was sitting on. She had to let out a sigh to calm the throbbing down.

"Oh shit, damn...my bad. Y'all can have a seat and it's plenty of liquor. Help yaselves and if you don't want this...Ming Si could get y'all what y'all want." Gallardo's eyes were still trained on Nikayla.

"Hey, big brother. We are here too," Gina cleared her throat. She was trying to be funny though.

"Hahaha very funny, sis. Where the rest of yo' clothes?" Gallardo grilled her, disapprovingly.

"Last I checked, I was grown." Gina laughed as she sat down next to Burnah.

"Yeah...get fucked up. You gets none of this liquor on this table. You already look lit. Here, drink this water." He passed her a water bottle from the table.

"Don't worry, sis. You can sip mine," GG licked her tongue at Gallardo and he rolled his eyes.

"So, wassup, Miss Lady?" Gallardo spoke to Nikayla as she danced in her seat.

The DJ had a strong 90s hip hop and R & B mix, in rotation.

"Nothing much, just trying to enjoy my night." Nikayla responded, with a small smirk on her face.

"Well, let me show you a good time." Gallardo gave her a sexy smile and it was so infectious, making her smile.

"Okay, fine."

The music had all of them dancing and looking like they were at some basement house party rather than in an upscale club. The rest of the night, the crew had fun and drank, danced, and laughed until the lights came on. They all decided to meet at the *IHOP* down the street and Gallardo demanded that Nikayla rode with him. She obliged his request, with no hesitation.

€€€€€€€

Girl you bets know how to fuckkkk baby
or to make loveee

The way you look...girlll you bets to know how
to fuck and to make love
The way you look
I know you know howww..

PARTYNEXTDOOR's smooth and eclectic voice blared through Gallardo's speaker system as he drove through Compton to *IHOP*. It was after the club and Nikayla was sitting on the passenger side vibing to the music. She was half past tipsy and Gallardo was feeling liquor that he consumed. He couldn't get over how captivating her beauty was. Those steel gray eyes of hers were so alluring. They drew you in and put you in a chokehold. Nikayla was a baddie and he needed her on his team. For now, he would play it slow and let her come to him. He knew she wouldn't be on his dick like the other girls. That went without saying.

"That's one of my favorite songs." Nikayla revealed, turning the radio down a little.

"Yeah, PartyNextDoor go hard as shit. He underrated like a motherfucker. I'll take him over Drake any day." Gallardo adjusted the hat on his head.

"I have to agree with you on that one. His music just have you so mellowed out."

"It delfinitely do." Gallardo concurred, as he pulled up in the IHOP parking lot, which was pretty packed.

Gallardo found a parking space and they headed in the restaurant. The crew was already there and already had two tables pushed together to seat all eight of them.

"What took y'all so long to get here," GG pried, looking at Gallardo and I with a skeptical look on her face.

"There was an accident on the shortcut I was taking from here. Chill ya little Inspector Gadget head ass out over there." Gallardo remarked, causing everyone at the table to laugh.

"Shut up!" Gretchen rolled her eyes at her brother.

"Well, since they here...can we order now?" KB looked up from his phone and asked.

"Yeah. Y'all didn't have to wait on me," Gallardo let them know.

"You don't have to tell me twice. Hey, you with the fat ass." KB called out to the waitress that was cleaning off another table.

She looked up at KB and rolled her eyes. She continued to clean the table she was working on.

"Ay, I'm ready to order and the customer is always right. That's why yo' ass lopsided now." KB was the type that would get mad and snap on a woman if he felt like he was being rejected.

"Look, I will be with you in a second. I'm trying to do my job." Everyone laughed and crowned him.

"Man, KB, why must you be rude to women?" GG asked him.

"Y'all hoes don't know y'all place. When a nigga speak, you bows the fuck down and do what he says!" KB snipped, followed by laughter from Zip and Burnah.

"Don't entertain his stupid ass!" GG spat, rolling her eyes at an unmoved KB.

After doing what she had to do, the waitress walked over to the table and let out a deep sigh of annoyance.

"Hey, my name is Thailand and I will be taking ya order. Would any of y'all like to try our new Cinnabon Pancakes or New York-Style Cheesecake pancakes tonight?" She had her pen and pad ready to take their orders.

"Naw, fuck all of that. Just bring me a Southwestern omelet and hold the pork, turkey bacon, and a side of pancakes. I want some orange juice too." Zip recited his order first.

Everyone else basically followed suit and she made sure that KB said his last.

"You gonna order or what?" Thailand was getting irritated with him.

"Yeah. Chill out with that stank ass attitude. I just want some oatmeal, fruit, and wheat bread. I want one of those sunrise drinks y'all got too." KB responded, deciding to give her a break from him being an asshole.

"I will be right back with y'all drinks and I'm putting these orders in." She walked away and KB's eyes were directly on her ass.

"Ugh, you're such an asshole!" GG griped and then went back to looking in her phone.

"She got a fat ass, so imma look. What the fuck you thought?" KB quipped, nonchalantly.

"Y'all can't get mad at bruh for doing what we supposed to do. I wouldn't look at any of y'all because y'all family, but I'm sure niggas be staring at all." Zip concurred with KB, not seeing anything wrong with what he did.

"Whatever." GG rolled her eyes at them again.

"Keep rolling them eyes and them bitches gonna get stuck, GG!" KB snapped at her, causing everyone to laugh.

They all knew that Gretchen was getting under his skin. That was one of his biggest pet peeves.

Nikayla was happy that she came out and she was enjoying everyone's company. She didn't mind hanging with them more and getting to know Gallardo better. She may be playing with fire when it comes to him, but she didn't care. She just wanted to carefree for a while. They finished their food and Gallardo picked up the tab. He did it without blanking an eye. He even left the waitress a hefty tip. After leaving the restaurant, they all stood outside, talking amongst themselves.

Gallardo and Nikayla stood near GG's car.

"Can I call you sometime?" Gallardo asked, adjusting the hat on his head.

"Hand me yo' phone." Nikayla held her hand out and he placed the Samsung Galaxy 7 Plus in her small palm.

Nikayla saved her phone number in his phone and passed it back.

"You know you gonna be mine one of these days, right?" He arched his eyebrows, challengingly.

"I'm not too sure about that, Mr. Gallardo." Nikayla smiled at him, though she was playing hard to get.

"You'll see. I'll show you better than I—," *POW! POW!* Gunshots ranged into the air and the men scrambled to decipher where they were coming from.

"GET DOWN ON THE GROUND! NOW!" Gallardo yelled out and pulled his guns from behind his back. He ran over to assist his crew in eliminating the threat to them.

Nikayla laid down on the ground, holding her ears to drown out the deafening sounds of glass shattering, people yelling, and shots ringing out. She was hoping that she made it out of this one. One thing was for sure, she was going to stay away from Gallardo if it was the last thing she was to ever do. She didn't want to spend her life dodging bullets. She had a son to live for. He only had one parent left and she couldn't do anything to place Naheem into danger. Choosing to be with this man or associated with him, seemed just like knocking on the Devil's door.

3

TRESS

*T*ress let himself into his grandparents' house. He sat at the table that was situated in the kitchen and noticed the stack of bills sitting there. He let out a deep sigh. It pained him that his grandparents wouldn't come to him for the money for his little sister, Tristan's medical bills, his little brother, Trayden's basketball gear or the mortgage of their house. Seeing the second red notice for the mortgage didn't sit well with him. He rifled through the large stack of mail and came across a letter from *UCLA*. He had been contemplating going back to school for his doctoral studies. He already had his Bachelors and a Masters degree in Architectural Studies and a minor in Business Management. He decided to re-enroll for his doctorate in Architecture. Tress was in the streets as the muscle for the *Black Mask Militia*, but he also owned an architectural firm. Architecture was his life and he love to perfect his craft. All of the men of the Black Mask Militia had something that they were good at and they had businesses outside of the illegal activity they partake in. The only one who wasn't trying to think about business was Burnah. He just wasn't trying to let the streets go. Even Zip was an auto mechanic at the companies they own from time to time.

Tress saw all of the other bills that were in the stack and placed them in his back pocket. He was going to pay them that day and leave some money on his brother and sister's bed. His grandfather, Jack was too proud to take any cash from him. Jack used to be a part of the Blood gang when he was younger, but decided to leave the life of banging when he got shot twenty years ago. He was only fifty-six and wanted to live longer than most gang members did. They were still pretty much young for them to be grandparents. Tress was only twenty-four and his mother was thirty-nine. She had him at fifteen, his brother, Trayden at twenty-two, and Tristan at twenty-four. After Tristan was hospitalized at the age of two for a sickle cell-related crisis, their mother picked up and disappeared from their lives. Since then, Jack and his wife, Audrey took care of them.

As he looked at the enrollment form from *UCLA*, his little sister, Tristan walked into the room. She was a really beautiful young lady. At fifteen, Tristan was 5'2 compared to Tress' 6'6 frame and Trayden's 6'2 frame. Tristan was a good girl who made straight As and had dreams of being a NBA basketball player. Tristan was stunning and still glowed despite her bouts with sickle cell. She still had a smile that would brighten up the room.

"Hey, Tress! What you doing here, big brother? I missed you." She gave him a hug and then headed back to the fridge.

"Wassup, sis. I missed you too. Where is Mameux and Poppadeaux?" He asked, referring to his grandparents.

"Did you forget that they were taking that seven-day cruise? They left this morning." Tristan remarked, looking at her brother for confirmation.

"Oh, shit. I forgot all about that." It truly slipped Tress' mind.

"You too young to be forgetting stuff like you do. Next, you're going to have a head full of gray hair." Tristan pointed out, jokingly.

"Very funny! Where's Tray?"

"Basketball practice. He gets out at six o' clock. I was supposed to go to my study hall, but I wasn't feeling well."

"You sure you good, lil sis? You need anything?" Tress was concerned about his sister's health and well-being.

"I'm okay...I just overextended myself at school today. I'm about to lie back down."

"Okay, lil one. Well, I'm about to get out of here. Call me if you feel worse or y'all need anything. Here's some money for you and Tray." Tress pulled out the stack of cash in his pocket and gave each of his siblings five hundred dollars apiece.

Tress left from the house and headed home to change clothes. He was headed up to *UCLA* so that he could sign up for classes. He was ready to see what his doctorate degree brought him. He knew he couldn't be in the streets forever, so his education would prepare him for life after all of the chaos and bullshit that he inflicted in Compton.

4

GG

*G*retchen sat in the study hall, trying to make sense of the Calculus 2 homework that her professor gave the class to do. She was in the library with her hair tied up in a messy bun, her glasses were on her eyes, and she was wearing a *Space Jam* baseball jersey, black leggings, and a pair of *Space Jam* Air Jordan 11s on her feet. She was biting on her mechanical pencil because this work was giving her a run for her money. She could easily say that this was the first time she ever felt like she may not pass a course.

As Gretchen was trying to wrap her mind around the course work, she smelled the familiar smell of Tom Ford Oud Wood cologne. She knew it was Tress and her heartbeat sped up a little. She had a deep crush on this man. Tress was fine as hell. He was 6'6, had caramel skin, had low cut curly hair, a full beard, and he was big and muscular. He was like a teddy bear. She fantasized about him many nights. She was using her fingers and her trusty bunny vibrator to get herself off. Tress was always sexy to her. She just wanted him to pick her up in his arms and give her the business. From seeing his print in some swimming trunks at her birthday party last year, she knew that he was packing. It was looking like a baby leg on his thigh. She never told Tress that she was feeling him and kept away because she knew how her brother and the rest of the crew got down. They all were certified manwhores. They fucked many women and didn't settle down. She didn't know much about Tress, except for he loved his family, had degrees, and was a part of the *Black Mask Militia.*

"Ay, wassup, GG?" Tress took a seat next to her.

"Hey, Tresshaun. What brings you up here?" Gretchen looked up from her math book to give him her full attention.

"I just enrolled back into school for the Spring. I saw you sitting in here, so I came to speak."

"Oh, that's wassup. I thought you were going to stop at yo' Masters."

"Yeah, I was...I just decided to go back because that Dr. in front of my name would be dope as fuck." Tress responded and they both shared a laugh.

"Shhhhh!" The librarian that was fixing books on the shelf admonished them for laughing and being too loud.

"Oh snap, let me chill before her mouse looking ass kick us out."

"Ohmigosh, shut up!" GG was holding in her laugh, so she wouldn't get kicked out.

"Why you in the library? Don't you got apartment-like dorm on campus?" Tress was curious because there was a lounge area in her dorm.

He knew that because it was himself and Gallardo that helped her move her stuff in, her freshman year. She had been staying in the same dorm-like apartment. Even though she wouldn't take money and stuff from him, her brother did pull a few strings for her to never change her room.

"This keeps me from blaring my music because I would be doing way more dancing than studying." Gretchen divulged to him, with a smile.

"Oh, I feel you. So, what you doing?" Tress inquired, looking at her for an answer.

"Calculus 2 and it is kicking my ass!" She griped, removing the glasses from her eyes and letting out a deep sigh.

"Let me see yo' book." He held his hands out for her to hand it to him.

Gretchen passed him the book and told him which problems she had to work on. Tress grabbed one of her pencils and a piece of paper. He showed her step-by-step how to do each problem. She was grateful for him and his skills at math.

"Ohmigosh! I appreciate you soooo much for helping me! Let me buy you some dinner to repay you." GG thanked him for his services.

"Well, shit, let's do it! A nigga would never turn down a meal." Tress smiled and accepted her token of appreciation.

"Where do you want to eat?" Gretchen asked, as she gather her things up to leave.

"You ever ate at *Wolfgang Puck Express*?" Tress queried, riding up from his seat.

"That's my shit! Now, you definitely got me hungry."

"Aight, let's go." Tress grabbed her backpack and they walked out of the library.

They walked side by side and headed to her dorm on the other side of campus. She needed to drop her bag off and change clothes. They made small talk as they walked around and GG spoke to a few people, including her sorors. She was a member of *Delta Sigma Theta*. After about ten minutes, they finally made it to the on-campus apartment that GG shared with Nikayla and her son, Naheem. When Gretchen unlocked the door, Naheem was sitting in the living room area, eating a snack and watching cartoon. He looked up and ran over to GG.

"Auntie, GG! Auntie GG!" He was always excited to see her.

"Hey, auntie's little man." Gretchen greeted him back with a big hug and kiss on the forehead.

"Who are you?" Naheem tried to puff his chest out like he was the man of the house.

"I'm Tress, lil homie. Nice to meet you." Tress bent down so he could dap Naheem up.

"Dammmnnn, you're tall!" Naheem shrieked, not realizing he slipped and cursed.

"Naheem, what have I told you about ya mouth! Go to ya room, NOW!" Nikayla emerged from the back and popped him in the back of the head.

"Ouch! Okay, mama. I'm sorry. See you later, Tress."

"Aight, see you later," Tress chortled, as Naheem ran to the back of the apartment.

Tress couldn't help, but laugh out loud because Naheem reminded him of himself when he was that age.

"Sorry about that, Tress. That boy think he is so grown."

"Naw, it's cool. Little man is funny as hell. So, what you up to?"

"Studying and about to cook in a few. Where y'all just came from?" Nikayla stared at GG, pointedly.

"None of ya business, hoe. Tress, I'll be out in a second once I change out of this that I have on. Make yourself at home." Gretchen replied and made her way to the back where her room was.

Nikayla followed behind her and closed the door. The rooms were soundproof, which was an added bonus of the apartments. She sat on the bed as GG began looking in her walk-in closet for something to wear.

"What you want, hoe?" GG feigned annoyance, as she focused on finding something to put on.

"What are y'all about to do? I thought you were pulling an all nighter at the library."

"I was at the library. I didn't have to be in there all night because Tress helped me with what I was struggling with. We are about to go get a bite to eat." Gretchen informed Nikayla, removing a pair of shoes from her top shelf and taking them to the bed.

"Getting study house calls and what not. Imma be like you when I grow up." Nikayla laughed and GG's face was priceless.

"Fuck you, Nik Nik!" Gretchen threw up her middle finger and joined her in laughing.

"Just bring me some food. You know Naheem's little ass is going to want pizza and a bitch will scream if she eats another slice!" Nikayla rolled her eyes, being her typical dramatic self.

"I got you."

"So, what's bothering you? Talk to mama." Gretchen looked at Tress and could see the stress written all over his face.

"My grandparents are drowning in debt due to my sister's medical bills, their mortgage, and the fact that my ol' man can't really find work. I'm stressing because they won't ask me for the money." Tress let out a deep sigh and took a sip of the water with lime he ordered.

"It will be alright. I'm sure you're going to pay it. You gotta understand that sometimes it's hard for people to come to others. Ya grandparents are strong folks. Give them some time and I'm sure they will come around." GG assured him, placing her hand on top of his.

"Yeah, I get that, but sometimes it just frustrates me that they would rather struggle than to let me pay them back for all of the years they put in for me."

"Things will get better." Gretchen smiled at him and squeezed his hand, gently.

"So, why haven't me and you ever went out on a date or anything like that?" Tress inquired, with a focused look on his face.

"You do know who my brother is, right?" GG looked at him to see if he was serious about what he just asked her.

"Of course I know who yo' brother is. Keeping shit real with you, I been asked the homie if I could date you. He just told me he would kill my ass if I fucked you over."

"Really?"

"Hell yeah. The rest of that shit is irrelevant. I wanna really see where shit go. I've been crushing on yo' little chocolate ass since we were young. You fine as fuck." Tress tucked his lips in between his teeth and had a glare of lust within his eyes.

"Damn, I thought I was the only one that was crushing."

"Naw, a nigga been heavy on you for a lil minute now. I just didn't make my move because you was with that mark ass nigga, Rick." Tress revealed, smiling and showing the diamond and golds in the top and bottom of his mouth.

He didn't wear his grill all the time. This was just one of those occasions that he had it in.

"Rick wasn't that bad. He was scared as hell of Gallardo and Zip. Other than that, he treated me well. He just was whack in bed....oh man, did I say that out loud." GG felt embarrassed for a second.

She was with Rick for a good year and some change. She endured the bad sex for that long. She actually had feelings for him, but found out Rick wasn't exactly being faithful to her. Fast forward six months and she was single as a dollar bill. Hearing that Tress was crushing, had her feeling like she was on cloud nine. Tress was 6'6, light like a PayDay bar, kept his facial hair trimmed into a full beard, wore his hair in that Dutch braid style, had dark bedroom eyes, and was built like a football player. She couldn't stop thinking about him, even as she sat at the table with him.

"Yeah, you did. That just tells me that you haven't been fucked like a real woman should be. Stick with me and I'll show you the great potential and power behind that pussy."

"I'll take ya word for it." Gretchen felt like she had a waterfall raining in her panties. Tress had her hot and bothered. She knew that he would make good on what he said. She wasn't even doubting that.

5

THAILAND

*A*fter a rough day of working at *IHOP*, Thai was tired and ready to go home. She was saving so she could get her car fixed and pay for her classes at *UCLA*. She could easily go to her parents for the money, but she would have to admit defeat. After she sided with her brothers, her parents cut herself and Henré off from the family's money. They denied her access to her bank account and the use of the Mercedes G-Wagon she usually drove. She could have easily called Buddah, Banks, Henré, or Bailey, but they had families and other responsibilities besides taking care of their spoiled little sister. Until she found a nursing job out here in LA, her job at IHOP was going to have to do. She got off the bus and was walking down Slauson Avenue to get to her apartment. Though LA was said to be notorious for drive-bys, robberies, and gang banging, Thailand didn't have a problem with it. She grew up in Philly in the suburbs, but most of her friends lived in the hood in South Philly, so she was used to hood shit. Besides the catcalls and the occasional staredowns, Thai hadn't run into any trouble.

Just as she was wiping the sweat from her brow and heading down another block, she heard a horn and music blaring. She looked to the left and it was the annoying dude from her shift that last week.

She rolled her eyes and kept walking. He let his window down and was holding on the horn.

"Ay, Yo, lil thickems! Why you gotta be like that with me?" KB chuckled, and stopped his car.

"I'm glad that you think that this is funny. If you would excuse me, I'm tired as hell and I just want to shower and get in my bed."

"Can I give you a ride?"

"I don't get in the car with strangers." Thailand replied, smartly and continued her trek home.

KB hopped out of the car and walked up so he could stand in front of Thailand. She finally looked up at him, since he was 6'1 to her 5'3 frame. Thailand thought he was sexy as hell. He was tall, dark like a Hershey's chocolate bar, had those unkempt and nappy freeform dreads at the top of his head and his sides were shaved down, with the sideburns connecting into his beard. He was dressed simply in a white t-shirt with a wife beater underneath, black Levi's jeans, and a pair of white and black Nike Cortezs that appeared to be fresh out of the box. He also wore a black shirt tied like a bandana on his head. He smelled really good and Thai wanted to know what kind of cologne it was that he was wearing.

"Can you move out of my way?" She rolled her eyes and tried to get past him.

"Chill out, girl. I'm trying to give you a ride as a peace offering and a nigga can see you sweating in this hot ass uniform." KB looked at her with his attention getting brown eyes.

"No, thank you," Thai dismissed his gesture, but deep down she really wanted to get in the car to cool down.

"Look, I'm not on any crazy shit. On me, let me just do this and I'll leave you alone." KB was being uncharacteristically kind, so Thai gave in so he would return to his normally rude demeanor.

"Uhhhh okay." Thailand relented and they walked back to the car.

KB pressed a button on the key fob in his hand and the doors popped open, without touching the door handle. Thailand had never seen anything like it before. She was kind of impressed with what she was seeing. He ran over to his side of the car and started it back up.

"Aren't you happy to get out that damn sun and off yo' feet?" KB asked, as he placed his car into gear.

"I mean, I guess so." *You don't know how good this feel*, Thailand mused to herself.

"Damn, you're a tough cookie to crack, girl. You hungry?"

"I could eat."

"I'm about to go fuck up some *Louis Burgers* though." KB rubbed his stomach and hit Thai with his award-winning smile.

They arrived at *Louis Burgers* and hit the drive-thru. KB ordered a bacon double cheeseburger, chili cheese fries, and a cherry limeade. Thai ordered a bacon cheeseburger and garden salad. Thailand gave him directions to her apartment and they headed up the stairs. KB was holding the food and her work bag. Thai opened the door and they walked into her apartment. She turned the air on and grabbed her bag from him.

" I'll be back in a few."

"Okay, I'm about to fuck this food up though." Thai headed to her room, so that she could shower and not smell so much like pancakes. That was one of the main things that she hated about working at *IHOP*. The food smells lingered on her. As she was showering, she heard the shower curtain move and the air sent a chill down her spine.

"What the hell are you doing?" Thailand rolled her neck and had this irritated look on her face.

"Something I should've done since the day I met yo' fine ass." KB removed his shirt and jeans. He was standing in front of her with just his boxer briefs.

"What's that?" She stared at him, shyly.

"Fuck the shit out of you." KB tore off his boxer briefs and hopped right in the shower with her.

He picked Thailand up and they engaged in a sensual tongue kiss. KB squeezed her ass and placed her back against the wall. She was surprised that he could pick her up. No other dude she ever been with was able to pick her up. She kissed and licked KB along his neck and chest. *This nigga gonna think I'm a thot*. Thai couldn't get that thought out of her head, but she wasn't going to stop what was happening between them. KB took his fingers and started exploring Thailand's pussy and almost burst just from feeling how wet and slick she was.

"Damn, that shit wet as fuck, yo. You gonna let me have that shit for real?" He looked her directly in the eyes.

"Yessssss," Thai moaned as he worked his fingers in and out of her, with precision.

"Say no more." KB entered her with one hard thrust.

He couldn't be patient after feeling how wet she was. Thailand's pussy felt like the inside of an aloe plant, wet, gushy, and sticky.

"Uhmmmmm!" Thai moaned out as KB just sat inside of her for a second, not moving.

"Damn, this shit is tight as fuck! Wowwwww! What the fuck? This shit tight like you are a virgin."

KB gazed up into her eyes and she avoided eye contact. She very much so was a virgin. In her twenty-one years, she hadn't slept with any man. The only thing close to sex she ever had was an ex eating her pussy. Most men assumed because Thailand was so curvaceous and feisty, that she was getting dick. They could be furthest from the truth. With a strict father like Barsdale Reynolds, Thai was not afforded much time to do much— that included losing her virginity.

"Shit! I never wanted to be the one to pop a girl's cherry. Y'all hoes get territorial afterwards. Fucccckkk!" KB growled and hit the shower wall, in frustration.

"Man, get ya disrespectful ass off of me, nigga!" Thailand pushed KB off of her and his dick exited her body with a pop.

"Me, disrespectful?! Yo' ass should've told me you were a virgin. Sitting up here acting like you get dick on a regular. I don't fuck bitches who don't know what they are doing. That shit ain't cool. I don't have time to teach ya ass how to fuck!"

"Now, I'm glad that I stopped you before this went too far! Get the fuck out of my house!" Thai yelled back at him, her face etched in anger.

Motherfucker, she thought to herself.

"With pleasure! Call me when you let some other nigga knock the rest of that cherry in." KB got out of the shower and grabbed his clothes from off the floor and exited the bathroom.

Though Thai didn't want to, she found herself crying on the bench that sat in her shower. She was pissed that she came across someone like KB. This was the worst first experience ever. Her lower body was throbbing, but all she could focus on was the fact that she thought she liked KB. Now, he repulsed her. There was no way around that.

6

MUNCHIE

"Take this dick!" Burnah yelled out, as he grabbed Gina's hair with what could be described as a death grip.

"Fuckkkk! Briiigggan, I'm about to cum again!" Gina screamed out, throwing it back faster against his dick.

She could feel her release about to come. They had been holed up in his house on and off for the last three days. He wanted to keep her safe and get in her guts as well. It had been a few days since the shooting at *IHOP* and they still didn't know who was gunning for them. Reluctantly, Gallardo gave in to Burnah being his sister's bodyguard while she was in town. He paid for a small detail while she was in Texas. They stayed there and were on call. He had no idea that they were fucking, but his reluctance came from the fact that Burnah was a wild nigga. Gallardo didn't like for his sisters to be around his street activity. The less they knew and were around, the better. The Feds would target anyone that they felt knew information whenever they had somebody under their radar. Having snitches like Doon on their team would have the Black Mask Militia on their radar soon and he wanted them nowhere near any of it. He brought nothing to his mother's doorstep as well.

If he knew that Burnah and his younger sister were involved, there would be hell to pay. They had been good at keeping things under wraps for now. Gina hadn't even told her sister that she messed with Burnah. She just pretended like it was a friendly crush. Though she knew that deep down, it was far more than she led on, for now she couldn't tell a soul. What was understood couldn't be explained is how Burnah explained it. Despite the bullets flying over their heads the other day, they didn't fear anything in the confines of Burnah's home in Long Beach.

"That's right! Squeeze that AI pussy against this dick, Munchie! Let that shit go like Daddy taught you." He smacked her against the thigh and ass.

"Agggghhhhh!" Gina let her juices from within rain down on Burnah like the money flows at *Magic City* in Atlanta on Mondays.

Burnah continued giving her deep strokes to get himself off. Gina tapped out because she bust a huge nut.

"Damnnnnn, why is this chocolate shit so motherfucking good?!" Burnah hollered out, as his semen splashed into the Trojan Magnum Ecstasy condom. He pulled out of Gina and was laid out from fatigue. She laid there and stared at the ceiling.

Once again, she danced with the idea of placing a label on what they had. She didn't want to argue again, so she kept those thoughts on her mind, to herself. Gina laid there and let sleep take over. She felt Burnah leave the bed, but didn't bother to open her eyes. He returned and cleaned between her legs ever so gently. She enjoyed the sensation, but didn't open her eyes. A small nap is what she needed to get her energy back. She succumbed to it and switched positions to her side. Burnah spooned behind her and she heard his light snoring in her ear. She welcomed the sound.

€€€€€€€

"Briggan, we gotta get out of this bed. We have been fucking for hours and I'm hungry," Gina whined, as he planted kisses on her neck and he poked her in the butt with his hard-on.

"Shit, you right. What you want to eat?" He let go of her waist and sat up.

"I haven't had *Fatburger* since I left LA for school. They definitely don't have any in Texas. Let's go get some." Gina rose up from the bed and headed to the bathroom to take care of her hygiene.

She turned around and saw Burnah stroking himself. She was tempted to get back in the bed with him and the rumpled sheets. Once she thought about how much her pussy throbbed from all the rounds they had been going, it was only a fleeting thought.

"See something you like," Burnah teased, as he stood, so she could get a closer look at his dick.

"Yes, I do. Too bad Ms. Kitty is out of commission right now." Gina revealed and turned back on her heels to trek to the bathroom.

Burnah watched the natural hypnotic sway of her hips and ass and couldn't help, but smile. He was in love, but didn't want to admit it. Gina loved him as well, but she wasn't sure that he would ever give up his philandering and hoeing ways. It was like he thrived on it. For all the love that she saw in his eyes, she felt sadness and pain as well. It hurt her that the man that she truly wanted in her life, couldn't let go of the thrill of having more that one conquest. This was the type of man that her daddy, Gallardo, her sister and mother warned her about. Still, she couldn't help that her heart yearned for Burnah. Briggan Nathaniel Hartfield was her heart. She just hatred the way that he treated her when it came to his dick. It was like he couldn't resist getting it wet, even to gain love.

Once Gina came out of the shower, she saw Burnah standing in his walk-in closet looking for something to wear. She admired his caramel skin, the fresh cut that had his waves on swim and his beard looking so healthy and sexy. Her eyes traveled to his chiseled abs and defined chest and she licked her lips as she thought about his bow legs and what was hidden by the gray towel he had wrapped around his waist. Burnah was working with a certified horse dick with cow balls. Gina used to be so scared of it when he first took her virginity, but now she couldn't get enough of it.

"Yo' ass better chill. You said you want something to eat, so get dressed before you be spread across my bed. Ogling me like a piece of meat is not free," he laughed and continued to search for something to wear.

"Boy, please! Wasn't nobody staring at you. You ain't even that cute." Gina playfully rolled her eyes and tried to hide the smile that was playing the corner of her lips.

"Keep trying to deny that shit. You know you can't get enough of me," Burnah replied, cockily as he grabbed his dick for emphasis.

Gina just sucked her teeth and focused on getting dressed. She didn't have time for his shenanigans, plus she felt an attitude coming on since she was hungry.

€€€€€€€

After eating *Fatburger*, they cruised around the streets with no destination in mind. Gina reached over and turned his radio down, earning her a mean mug and she just chuckled.

"Briggan, can you run me by Deena's shop, so I can get my nails and toes done? Plllleeeeeaaassee!" She gave him her puppy dog eyes.

"Munchie, chill with that. I'll drop ya ass off. A nigga gotta go handle some business anyway." Burnah made an U-Turn and headed to Deena's shop.

He dropped Gina off and went to handle whatever business he had to. Gina strutted into the nail salon and greeted everyone that she knew. She noticed a few of the women giving her the cold shoulder, but ignored it. She knew that it probably had something to do with Burnah and his inability to keep his dick in his pants.

ONCE GINA'S nails and toes were finished, she went to go sit at one of the drying stations. She texted Burnah and let him know that she was ready. Once her nails were dry, she reached over and grabbed one of the magazines from the stand beside her. She couldn't help but notice two girls mugging her and trying to whisper. They were a hot ghetto mess if you asked Gina. She ignored them and continued to try and tune them out.

"Girl, Burnah's sexy ass put it down on me last night. Nigga had me speaking in tongues!" The loud and rambunctious girl slapped hands with her cackling friend.

She was telling her friend of her exploits with Burnah. Gina knew that she was trying to be messy because she saw him drop her off. Gina sat there and continued to read the magazine, not even reading into the mess. Bitches love to be seen and heard. She thought to herself, rolling her eyes.

"Damn, what did you do?" The friend looked over at Gina for a second.

"What you mean what did, I rode that dick like a low rider in a Dr. Dre video! It was goodddd!" They continued their little cackling fest and Burnah walked into the nail salon.

Gina had a grimace on her face and if looks could kill, he would be casket bound.

Her resolve almost melted because he walked in looking good enough to eat. Burnah was wearing white tee, dark blue Levi's, and black and white Chucks on his feet. He also wore a Cuban link necklace, a Cartier watch, and black LA Dodgers hat. Burnah was bowlegged, so he swaggered over to her, paying no attention to the eyes and whispering around him.

"Ay, you ready? I'm hungry as fuck." He stared at Gina, wondering why she had this mean mug on her face.

"Yeah," she replied, dryly.

"What the fuck is yo' problem, Munchie? We was just cool before I dropped you off. I swear you stay tripping on me."

Gina didn't say any further words out of her mouth. She just gathered her purse and walked out the door. She walked past Burnah's car and he stopped to see what the hell she was doing.

"Munchie, what the fuck is wrong with you for real? I'm not going to ask yo lil ass again." He snipped, through gritted teeth.

"That funky bitch inside of the salon was talking about how you fucked her last night with her messy ass!"

"Who? Paige? Yeah, the fuck right! She let the little homies run a train and bust on her face last night. I came through and kicked their asses because they was fucking on the job." Burnah explained to her.

"Well, she was in there telling her friend you had her speaking in tongues and shit!" Gina was still trying to be mad at him.

"She ain't fuck me...matter of fact, hold up." Burnah sped back into the nail salon, with a purpose in his walk.

Gina followed behind him to see what he was doing. BANG! Burnah opened up the door and it slammed against the glass behind it, alerting everyone of his presence. The door and window now had a crack in it, but he didn't care. The owner, Dena wasn't going for that though.

"Burnah, you're going to pay for my shit! I don't care how mad you are!" She yelled out, in annoyance.

"My fault, Dee. I gotcha." He assured her as he walked over to the two women who were talking mess in while Gina was in earshot.

Without warning, Burnah yoked the girl out of her seat. She was a pretty redbone with an awesome shape. She kind of put you in the mindset of a lighter skinned Miracle Watts. She was Burnah's type, and she would've believed the girl before hearing from him. She felt stupid for even getting mad about what she heard.

"Burnah...why...why...you grabbing me like this?" The girl who was basically bragging about sleeping with him, managed to yelp.

"Bitch, why you out here lying on me? Talking about you fucked me last night!" Burnah snapped, still yoking her against the wall.

All of the women in the shop were watching, in pure shock. They all didn't know what was unfolding before their eyes, but they were here for it. It was just like another day in the life of salon patrons. They saw drama almost everyday like it was tea time at an elite country club or high society meeting. Everything from cheating baby-daddies, who was fucking who's husband or what new baller was snagged circulated through these walls. It was like a ghetto *TMZ* or *Mediatakeout* in there. Deena, the owner was ratchet so she didn't mind the drama taking place. All she asked is that her shop didn't get damaged in the process. She took pride in her shop. She was

Burnah's mother's best friend at one point and took care of him. Burnah was best friends with her son, PJ, but he got shot down on *Crenshaw Boulevard* during a dice game.

"I didn't...I didn't say that." She tried to lie her way out of it, but Burnah wasn't trying to hear that.

"Naw, you slimy bitch, you lying! You let the lil homies rock that loose, ran through pussy last night," her eyes bugged out from both surprise and embarrassment. They told her that they would keep it to themselves and they were having fun. "Don't look so shocked now. They recorded everything you did. They was going to put ya simple ass on Facebook, but I took the video from them." Burnah chastised her, not feeling any bit of remorse for eating her dirty laundry to the females in the salon.

There were three who he personally paid visits to, but they knew about Gina. He told them straight up what it was and they played their positions. That was why he never gave Paige the dick. She didn't know what the word discretion meant. Burnah wanted to see what she was hitting on, but he was glad the young homies showed him what kind of girl she really was. She was another one on the long list of pass arounds in the city.

Without further conversation, Burnah dropped a stack on Deena's receptionist table and headed out of the nail salon, with Gina in tow.

That day, they continued to smoke, argue and fuck. It was all starting to become routine for Gina and she was tired of it. All she wanted to do was be with Burnah and not have to worry about this girl and that girl.

7

BURNAH

*S*ince the night of the club and *IHOP* incident, Burnah had been more vigilant than normal. He wasn't taking any chances on something happening to the crew. In the grand scheme of things, they were the only family that he had. Burnah was a loner. His mother lived in Skid Row, but he had no type of communication with her. As long as she chose coke and PCP over him, there was no room for her in his life. The only one who knew more about his life than anyone was Gina. The day before Munchie left played in his head over and over. Right now, he didn't even know if they had a friendship. Though he could see himself spending the rest of his days with her, it was just something about commitment that made Burnah run for the hills and never look back.

"Briggan, why can't we be together? I'm tired of all of the same mundane bullshit between us." Gina griped, placing her head up against the headboard.

They had been fucking and fighting all day. Burnah studied her naked, sweat-laden body in deep admiration. She was his chocolate drop and no one else's. He just hated that she wouldn't leave well enough, alone. His dick softened like a gummy worm in the hot sun.

He was turned off by the conversation they were having. She was beating the hell out of a dead horse.

"Not right now, Munchie. You gotta give me some time. Shit ain't that simple, baby."

"You know what? I'm sick of the same ol' shit with you. I'm gone! Don't try to call or text me! I mean it this time!" Gina rose from the bed and ran to the bathroom.

He knew that she was most likely crying. I love this damn girl, but that monogamy shit ain't for me.

Burnah's phone went off alerting him to a text. It was a text from one of his freak hoes, Nandi. He smiled as he read the text and saw the picture attached.

Nandi: Can't wait for you to come and handle this. She's been missing you.

The picture of Nandi playing with her self and her pussy was glistening.

Burnah: Damn. That shit look good as fuck. Once I finish up my business, I be through. Make a nigga some food. I don't feel like eating that fast food shit.

Burnah placed his phone on his nightstand and laid his head back on the bed of crumpled sheets. The sheets smelled like a mix of Gina's Gucci perfume, Burnah's Christian Louboutin cologne, Blueberry AK-47 Kush, and sex. He closed his eyes and just laid there, in deep thought. He knew he couldn't keep playing with Gina's heart, but committing to her wasn't an option right now, either.

Gina walked out the bathroom, fully dressed and her face full of strife and sadness.

"After tonight you don't have to worry about me!" She replied, gathering up her overnight bag, keys, and cellphone.

"Man, Munchie, chill out." Burnah rose up from the bed and walked over to her.

"Ain't no chill. I'm done with this shit. You been stringing me along for four years and I just have you my virginity last year! I'm done!" Gina tried to walk away, but he grabbed into a bear hug from behind.

"I keep telling ya ass that this shit just not that simple!" Burnah's voice boomed, echoing throughout the room.

"That's what you keep saying and I don't care! When I get on that plane for Texas tomorrow morning...this here is a wrap. It's just that simple!" Burnah let her go and Gina sauntered out of his room and left just as quietly as she came in.

Burnah let out a deep sigh. He couldn't run after her if he wanted to. His pride wouldn't let him. That's just the way that it was. As he drove around to check out the traps, he knew he would have to reach out to Gina, but now was not the time. He had to focus on his paper and the *Black Mask Militia*.

€€€€€€€

Burnah sat in the trap house and counted the earnings for the day. He didn't trust anyone, so he rode around and made sure everyone was on their Ps and Qs. Burnah was the wildest out of the whole crew. He was also the youngest. He'd just turned twenty-one and he had no intentions of turning his life of crime around. Burnah was born in the poverty-stricken, violent streets of Kingston, Jamaica. He still had his accent, but that's the only thing that connected him to the country. He had been living in Los Angeles since he was eight years old. His mother was a prostitute and her pimp moved them to another country and city. Once his mother turned to drugs when he was fifteen, Burnah was basically left to fend for himself. That was when he officially became a part of the BMM.

He was reclusive and never told anyone about his life or let anyone into his world. He was not the committing type, but lately he'd been feeling things for Gallardo's sister, Gina. He took Gina's virginity a year ago. Despite doing that, he couldn't leave the girls in the streets alone. It was like they had a strong hold on him. They kept their exploits a secret from everyone else. Burnah was sure that Gallardo would try to knock his head off. He was overprotective of his little sisters. He kept a tight eye on Munchie the most. She was nineteen and gone off to school at *Gramblimg State* in Texas. Burnah didn't feel like he was capable of a long-distance relationship, so that was another reason why he wasn't trying to go there with Gina either. She was everything that he needed, but he knew that he couldn't give her what she wanted until he got finished with this hoe phase. A man will never be ready to settle down with one girl until he is matured and willing to do it. Plenty of girls have tried to lock Burnah down, but he wasn't with it.

"Y'all niggas lucky that it is all there. I'll see y'all later on when I drop the re-up to the house." Burnah picked up the duffle bags and left out of the door.

He was ready to go to sleep. It was like eleven o' clock at night and since he's been up for like two days off of coke and Xannys, Gallardo told him to go home and get some rest. As he opened the trunk of his Tesla, he heard gunshots. That was normal for Lynwood though, so he wasn't alarmed. He placed the bags in the trunk and closed it. As he was heading to the drivers' side, he was attacked by a shadowy figure. He was bust upside the head with the butt of a gun. Burnah hit the ground and let out a grunt as his arm scratched against the asphalt and the skin peeled off, from the impact of his fall.

"Man...ahhh fuccckkk! What y'all niggas want?"

"This ain't no riddle, cuh! Give me the money for I kill yo bitch ass!"

"Nigga, you real funny!" Burnah let out a hearty laugh, despite the pain that he was feeling from his raw arm.

It was bleeding all over the place too.

"You think this a game, nigga?!" The dude yelled, gruffly.

"You a joke!" Burnah stood there and stared at the masked man, with no fear in his eyes.

Burnah wasn't the type to fear death. He welcomed it. If he was going to die. He was going to have some fun before he took his last breath. Now, that he thought about it. The gunshots did sound close, so now he knew this to be a jack move.

"Fuck you, nigga!" The masked man was getting pissed off.

Unbeknownst to Burnah, this was his first time robbing someone. He was helping his cousin get back at the *Black Mask Militia* for killing him. They sent his body parts to several members of the family. Lathan felt like Doon was a bitch nigga, but at the end of the day he was family. Blood was thicker than any of the shit in life. Lathan was a Crip and was chancing his life either way to avenge his cousin. It was him and three of his crew members, Crazy Man, Cannon, and Creem. They knew that the Black Mask Militia was ruthless and Blood gang-affiliated. Their lives were hanging on a balance from many angles.

"Fuck is you, Jim Carrey? Open the fucking trunk or I'm blowing ya shit out here!"

"I can tell you an amateur at this shit. Ya other niggas left ya bitch ass out here." Without any warning, Burnah started inching toward Lathan to attack.

The fear was imminent on Lathan, so he decided to bust his gun before Burnah could get ahold of him. Burnah felt holes burning through his body, but the adrenaline was still rushing through his veins. He managed to knock the gun out of Lathan's hand and tackle him to the ground. As they scrambled to get to their feet, Burnah started feeling lightheaded and his body gave into the darkness. He laid unconscious, leaking blood profusely from the gaping gunshot wounds on his body.

8

ZIP

Zip rode down the LA streets bumping YG. He was headed to his babymother, Saya's house to see his daughter, Zasaya. She hadn't seen his face in like two months, due to the games that her mother played. That bitter baby mama thing fit Saya to the tee. She made Zip's life a living hell because he didn't want to be with her. He had his reasons why things would never work between them. Saya just couldn't accept it and move on with her life. There was a time that he loved her, but that ship sailed a long time ago. Zacarion was young, wild, free and single. His only focus was his money and taking care of his child. He parked in her gated apartment complex and turned his engine off. He was a little high, but he needed something to keep the edge off. He always envisioned himself choking the life out of her, so he needed something to prevent that at all costs. Zip walked up to her apartment and knocked.

KNOCK! KNOCK! BAM!

"Who is that banging at my motherfucking door?" Saya yelled out, in her typical ghetto manner.

"Girl, open this damn door," Zip called out, feeling himself already getting mad.

"Nigga, I don't care who you are. Don't be banging at my door! Now, what the hell do you want?" Saya replied smartly, as she swung the door open.

"Not yo' ass! Where the fuck is Zasaya at, man?"

"She at her grandma house. Now, you worried about my baby? You not about to be a part time daddy, so I'm keeping her away!" Saya rolled her neck and rolled her eyes.

"Bitch, you crazy if you think you're going to keep, keeping my daughter away from me! I left yo' trifling ass, not Zasaya!" Zip yelled, feeling his temper about to erupt.

"How many times do I have to say I'm sorry? Rodney was a mistake. You were never here and you were out here having fun with every bitch that would smile in ya face." Zip ex-girlfriend and baby-mother, Saya cried, tears flowing down her eyes like a waterfall.

"I don't wanna hear that shit. None of them bitches mattered and they wasn't yo' friends either. You fucked one of my workers and this nigga tried to clown me. Ain't no coming back from that shit, Saya. I don't care what you say."

"Ohmigod! Why does everything have to be about you?! You decided to place everything above me and I was lonely."

"Why not tell me that shit? You nagged me about everything else! Now, you wanna play victim and act like I'm supposed to give you some type of sympathy or hall pass! I'm done with this conversation with you. I got some shit to handle. I will be picking up my daughter from yo' mama house."

"Fuck you, Zacarion !" Saya yelled, but it fell on deaf ears because Zip slammed the door and went back to his car.

Zip jumped into his car and headed to the trap house they had in Carson. As he was riding, he lit the rest of the joint he had because Saya had him pissed. The crazy thing was that before all this happened, Zip would've put a ring on her finger. Now, he couldn't even look at her. He didn't tell Saya that he knew that Rodney asked her to let him and a few of his niggas run a train on her. They recorded it and was watching it in the trap one day. That disgusted him. He didn't even understand why she did it. He gave Saya everything she needed. Yeah, he fucked with other women from time to time, but none of them could say that they got the same treatment as her. Now, all he did was pay his child support and Saya's rent to make sure that his daughter had a roof over her head. He wanted to get her full time, but he had felonies and was too deep in the street life. He didn't feel that there was a judge in LA County that would grant him sole custody.

€€€€€€€

Zip decided to grab some *4J's Wood Pit BBQ* on his way back to the hood. He was hungry as hell and could almost taste the food. He had the munchies like a motherfucker too. As he was parking, he saw his ex-best friend, Suri heading into the restaurant. Suri was the best friend that a man could ask for. Zip never saw her as a piece of meat like he did other women. He treated Suri like a sister. They were cool up until he got Saya pregnant. Saya and Suri never liked each other and being head over heels, Zip chose his relationship over his friendship.

He hadn't seen her in about four years because she moved out to New York. Suri was always a beautiful woman, but looking at her now, Zip could see that her body went through some changes. Suri was thick in all the right places, she didn't wear her glasses anymore and she didn't have on the baggy clothes. Right now, she was wearing a pair of pair of overalls, a red crop top, and a pair of all red Adidas on her feet.

"Suri Uri got a fatty now! Let me find out!" Zip hollered out before she made it into the restaurant.

Suri turned around to see who it was. She had an idea that it was Zip. He was the only one who called her Suri Uri. She was lowkey still a little mad at him for choosing Saya over her. She knew that she was pregnant at the time, but Suri really liked Zip. Of course she never told him, but in her mind she felt like he should have known how she felt.

"Hey, Zacarion." She forced herself not to curse him out.

"Damn, you still mad at a nigga, huh?"

"Why you say that?" She scrunched her nose up at him and avoided eye contact.

"Usually you call a nigga, Ziploc or that corny ass bestie shit." Zip pointed out, with a smile.

"Well, I don't know what you're calling yourself these days. I haven't seen you in four years."

"Imma drop that...how you been though? How is New York?"

"I've been pretty good. New York is great, but I decided to transfer back home, since my mother is sick." Suri responded, finally making eye contact.

"Yeah, I'm sure that yo' moms would dig that. I went to see her a few days ago. She ain't looking too good, but her spirit is high as ever."

" Yeah, my ol' girl is being strong. How is Saya and ya daughter?"

"Saya the same hoe she always been...no sugar coating that. Zasaya is six going on twenty-six. That's my baby, though." Zip was filled with a sense of pride whenever he talked about his daughter. Zasaya was the best thing to ever happen to him, in spite of the tumultuous relationship he had with her mother.

"That's wassup. Well, I'm grabbing me something to eat before I have to head back to work."

"I'm grabbing me some shit because I got the munchies like a motherfucker." Zip chuckled, as they both walked to go in the restaurant.

His was red as the Devil's dick and they were low. When Zip got high, he smoked the best that California had to offer. That stuff straight from Mexico. Their connect, Andelé had that pure gas and any other drug that was poppin in the streets.

"You know what you're ordering?" Zip inquired, as he looked at the menu.

"You should know what I want." Suri responded, putting him to the test.

"Ah, shit...how can I forget?" Zip let out a chuckle and started ordering both of their food orders.

"Ay, I saw Suri today, bruh." Zip blurted, as they sat in Gallardo's house watching *SportsCenter*.

"Damn. Talk about a blast from the past. How she look? She still look the same?" Gallardo took a sip of the bottle of Fiji water he was drinking.

"She look fine as fuck. I know she was kinda playing a nigga to the left. She did give me her number though."

"So, you gonna try to make a move in on that? She the only chick I know that you let friend zone yo' ass." Gallardo laughed, loudly.

"Fuck you," Zip shot his middle finger up at his cousin.

"I'm serious though. All the females we done fucked...some of the same ones, she was the only one who decided that y'all wouldn't take it there. Then you chose Saya over her. I just always found that to be odd."

"Yeah. Well, I knew she was a good girl and I wasn't trying to fuck her over. Being that she was not a bop, shit would've been sketchy from the get go. Had I got with Suri, she would be sucked in this life. I couldn't have that happen. Her mama raised her right. Even now, I don't think that I could make that happen. I'm deep in this shit and don't feel that changing anytime soon."

"I feel you on that, but we gonna have to chill because niggas like Doon exist all across the boards and we can't end up like my dad and them."

"I hear what you saying, but the game is in my blood. I don't know if I can walk away from it. Honestly, I feel like I will be in it until my casket drop." Zip revealed, honestly, taking a sip of the Corona in his hand.

"Just make sure you have some plays in place before shit be too late. Don't end up like pop and unc."

"Yeah, I hear ya, bruh. I just got some thinking to do." Zip let out a deep sigh and closed his eyes, so he could rub his temples.

Later that night, Zip found himself heading to South Gate to get some *In-N-Out Burger*. He was craving a double bacon cheeseburger with Animal fries. His stomach was growling just from the thought of it. He smoked his rolled joint and listened to YG's *Still Brazy*. The music blared from his speakers. His mind was on what Gallardo said to him. He knew he had to get out of the game, but that easier said than done. This lifestyle was in his blood. It was just the way that life went.

Zip made it to the restaurant and parked his car. He hopped out and walked into the restaurant. As he was standing in line for his food, he heard a familiar laugh. He looked behind him and saw Suri sitting at a table with her mother and her little, sister, Morgan. Zip eyes focused on Suri and she was wearing an Adidas crop top and matching capris. Her tattoos were on full display, including the boss ass *Compton Made* tat she had on abdomen. They both had the same tattoo, but hers was sexy as hell. On her feet, was a pair of white Yeezy 360 Boosts. He focused in on her beautiful face and her long, curly tresses. His dick was fighting a battle of getting hard in the middle of the restaurant. He buttoned up the Los Angeles Raiders jersey to be respectful of Suri's mother, Ms. Stephanie and pulled his pants up, as well. He walked over to them and they smelled his Kush and cologne before he even made it to the table.

"Ay, wassup?" Zip greeted the table.

"Wassup, Zip," Morgan jumped up and gave him a hug.

"Hello, Zacarion. I was just asking Suri if she saw you, yet." Ms. Stephanie smiled at him.

"Yeah...we saw each other earlier when I pulled up to grab something to eat. Now, I'm grabbing some food, so I can head home."

"It was nice seeing you, baby." Ms. Stephanie was trying to stand, but Zip hugged her while she was sitting.

"Don't strain yourself, Ms. Stephanie." Zip smiled and placed a kiss on her forehead.

He felt Suri's eyes on him, but he was focused on her mother at the moment. She had breast cancer and it was in remission at some point. It came back worse than before. Lately, chemotherapy was kicking her ass, but her spirit was still divine. Zip admired that and felt like she was his mother. She was there for him when his mother decided to leave and he never hear anything from her.

"I'm okay, Zacarion. Suri is cooking Sunday dinner...you should come over." Zip looked up at Suri and she rolled her eyes.

"I may come through. Well, I'm going to leave you all back to yo' dinner. See you all later."

"Bye, Zacarion," they all replied, in unison.

€€€€€€€

Zip headed back into the line, so that he can order his food. He was hungry as hell and tempted to eat in the restaurant. He decided against that because he was sure that Suri would be on that good bullshit. Zip knew she was probably still mad at him, so he was going to just fall back. He walked out of the restaurant and headed to his home in Long Beach. He decided to leave his daughter with her grandmother and pick her up first thing in the morning. The only thing on his mental besides his daughter, was the Suri situation and his money. He knew he had to have her, but that would be easier said than done.

As Zip was turning into his driveway, his phone chimed to indicate that he had a message. It also did that strong ass vibration that iPhones have. He turned his car off and grabbed his food. He would check his messages once he started eating. He got out of the car and checked his surroundings. In the line of work that he was in, he couldn't afford to slip up. Plus, they just dealt with somebody shooting at them at *IHOP*. That was a crazy night/ morning all in itself. He walked in his house and disarmed the alarm. He rearmed it and walked to his kitchen. Placing all of his stuff on the counter, he went into his refrigerator and grabbed a bottle of Vitaminwater XXX from the shelf. He poured the contents into a cup and grabbed his food and phone. He kicked off his shoes and grabbed the remote to turn on the TV.

Once he started eating and settled for some movie, he finally picked up his phone. He had a text from Suri and an unknown number. He figured that it was one of his freaks. He skipped that message and went to Suri's

> **Suri Uri: It was nice to see you.**
> **Zip: yea it was cool seeing u and yo' folks.**
> **Suri Uri: I missed you when I was gone.**
> **Zip: I missed u too. Can I take u out and shit?**

SURI URI: JUST LET ME KNOW WHEN
ZIP: I GOTCHA.

Suri Uri: Well, I'm about to get some sleep since I have to wake up early. See you Sunday.
Zip: aight see u then.

Zip put his phone down and it chimed again. It was from the same unknown number from before. He opened the message and was immediately pissed off. He flipped over his coffee table and glass flew everywhere.

"What the fuck?!" He yelled out, full of anger.

He was sent a video of Burnah being gunned down at one of their traps. The shit had him ready to go on a warpath. He immediately called KB. KB answered on the third ring.

"Ay, my nigga, wassup?" KB replied groggily, rubbing the sleep out of his eyes.

"Shit is crazy! Motherfuckers gotta feel us out here! Niggas sent me a video of Burnah getting murked in front of the trap!" He was pacing the floor by then, now caring about the glass since he had on Nike slides.

"What the fuck? Not my nigga!" KB was fully alert and throwing on some clothes.

"This shit got me on go mode. Meet me in Lynwood!" Zip hung up the phone and grabbed his keys so he could drive to Lynwood. This shit was not good. They couldn't afford any of these attacks that have been hitting them lately. They had to get the reigns on this quick before niggas really be gunning for them.

9

KB

*A*rriving at the trap house on Lynwood, KB found it teeming with one time cars and crime tape. There was a crowd standing around. He stood within the crowd and tried to blend in. He needed to know what happened and needed to know fast. This shooting hit too close to home. Their crew was not known to be sloppy. He notice the neighborhood information girl, Anjee standing off to the side. She was a basehead and drunk, but she knew what the hell she was talking about. Anything you wanted to know Anjee had the word for a small amount of drugs or a few dollars in her pocket. KB moved through the crowd of onlookers and made his way over to her. Anjee was shivering from the drop in temperature that the nights in LA brought. KB wore a hoodie, so he took it off and passed it to her.

"Ay, Anjee, what went down out here?"

"Let's go down the block. These motherfucking pigs are nosy and I ain't Muslim," she snipped, with a look of disgust on her face.

They walked further down the block, to the stop sign that was riddled with bullets. The street wasn't lit properly due to hustlers and street kids busting out the streetlights.

"So, what you got for me?" KB got straight to the point.

Though Anjee was cool, she still had that smell of armpit sweat, outdoor, and urine reeking from her body. KB felt the food he ate, threatening to come up and empty all over the sidewalk. He didn't want to judge her, but Anjee needed to get herself together.

"What you got for me, KB? I know you got that good shit!" She yelped excitedly, showing off the little bit of teeth she had in her mouth.

They were yellow and black. The teeth were decaying in her mouth. When she smiled, it made her look like she was like eighty instead of thirty four.

"Here." KB pulled out three crisp one hundred dollar bills and placed it in her hand.

Anjee pocketed the money extra fast, in case KB decided to change his mind at any second.

"Three masked niggas kicked in the doors of the trap and killed y'all boys and shot up Burnah. Heard one of the dudes say it was revenge for Lathan. They Crips." Anjee relayed the information to him.

KB felt his nostrils flaring and he was consumed with anger. Just before he could speak to Anjee some more, his cellphone rang. It was Zip calling him.

"Aye, wassup, bruh." KB spoke into the phone.

"Where you at? I'm at the spot...had to park on the street over."

"At the end of the block with Anjee. Roll up on me real fast."

"I gotcha." They hung up the phone and Zip came walking up the block.

KB relayed all of the information that Anjee told him and they headed to *St. Francis Medical Center.* That was the hospital that was the closest to the trap.

KB and Zip rode in silence, besides when they were on the phone with the rest of the crew.

€€€€€€€

Once they arrived at the hospital, Gallardo, GG, and Tress were in the waiting room. Gallardo was pacing, in deep agitation. He hated that Burnah was sitting in the hospital just like he would hate if it was anyone else in the Militia.

"What's up with the homie?" Zip walked up to Tress and asked.

"He's in surgery right now and we are waiting for the doctor to come through." Tress informed him.

"Damn. One Time came through sniffing around, yet?" Zip inquired, looking at Tress.

"Naw, but I'm sure that they will be here at any minute. This shit is crazy because they ran up in the trap like this was an inside job or some shit."

"We will talk about this later, but Anjee ass gave us some science when we ran up on her."

"Aight, well, I guess we all will just wait."

KB went and sat at a seat. He found himself thinking about Thailand and the way things went with her. He just couldn't himself being with a virgin, but at the same time he wanted her. The way her pussy felt against his dick had him about to lose his mind. KB had a soft spot for the girl and couldn't deny it if he wanted to. He grabbed his phone and decided to text her.

KB: WYD?

He sat down and waited for a response. He caught some highlights of sports on ESPN.com and browsed his Instagram. It was the only social media app that he had. He looked at all of the women down his timeline and the many DMs that he had. Some were of women showing him pussy shots, some asking when he was going to come fuck them again, and others were trying to throw pussy at him. KB laughed and continued looking at his page. He was growing impatient that Thai hadn't respond to him yet.

KB: U KNOW U SEEN MY TEXT

KB: WHY YOU NOT RESPONDING?

KB: Wyd? Don't make me roll up on you.
KB: You think this is a game?
KB: You better answer me.

KB put his phone down and waited for her to message him back. He knew that she would once he blew her phone up. A few seconds later, KB's cellphone chimed, letting him know that he had a message. He smiled when he saw Thailand texted back.

Thai: Can you stop texting me? I thought we didn't have anything to talk about.

KB: WHY YOU BRINGING UP OLD SHIT?

THAI: UGH! LEAVE ME ALONE, KB.

KB: I asked you what you were doing?
Thai: I'm at work, so leave me alone.
KB: You a virgin stripper and pancake maker?

THAI: FUCK YOU!

KB: YOU COULD BE A LITTLE NICER.

KB placed his phone in his pocket when he saw the doctor and the nurse walk up on them. He stood in his seat and went to stand with everyone else. When he saw Thailand standing there, he had a big smirk on his face. She rolled her eyes, in response to his smirk.

"Hi, I'm Dr. McHenry and this is my nurse, Thailand. We will be taking care of Briggan while he was here. The surgery was a success. Briggan was shot five times, once in the head, twice in the hip, once in the thigh, and once in the foot. The good news about the situation is that four of the five bullets were grazes. The bullet to the hip was the only one that was severe. Mr. Hartfield will have to go through some extensive physical therapy to be able to walk. Other than that, Mr. Hartfield is a lucky man." The doctor shared this information with them. They all were quiet and letting the information set in.

"Can we go see him?" GG asked Dr. McHenry, wondering if his boy was gonna be okay.

"Yes, you can. I will have Thailand hold off on giving him any medicine, until you guys leave. He is in room 1245. You all have a nice night." Himself and Thailand walked off, with KB watching her ass in lust.

"Nigga, ain't that the girl from *IHOP*?" Zip looked over to KB, in confusion.

"Yeah, that's her little mean ass."

"Why she looked at you like that? What did you do, KB?" GG hit him on the back of the head.

"Ay, chill with yo damn hands, GG! I didn't do shit to that female...shit was just brazy with us." KB let out a sigh and he noticed that Thailand went into the bathroom.

He excused himself and went into the direction where he saw her go. He went into the bathroom and locked the door behind him. Thai was in the stall taking care of her business. He stood off to the side and waited for her to come out. The toilet flushed and she opened the stall. Not paying attention, she pushed the soap dispenser and distributed some on her hand. She turned the water on and washed her hands.

€€€€€€€

Once she looked up, you could tell that KB scared the living daylights out of her.

"Oh, shit! You scared the hell out of me!" She clutched her chest and rolled her eyes.

"Shut up." KB growled and walked up behind her.

"Man, gone on about ya business. I'm not about to play with you. You said all that you had to say in my bathroom." Thailand was not trying to hear what he had to say.

"You still mad at me?" KB licked her neck and placed his rock hard dick against her ass.

"KB, move!" She took her elbow and drove it into his torso.

"My name is Kashim and you about to be screaming that shit, right now." KB growled through clenched teeth.

He took his hand and placed it inside of her scrubs. He played with her clit and was in awe at how wet she was.

"KB, don't do this. I just got this job." Thai moaned, from the sensations that he was sending through her body.

"You told me that like I give a fuck.

KB took his hands and pulled down her scrub bottoms and the thong she was wearing. Kneeling down, he started eating her pussy from the back. He usually didn't do that, but he knew Thai was untouched and her pussy was glistening like a glazed donut. He couldn't resist the urge to put it in his mouth.

"Uhmmmm!" Thai moaned, softly.

She was delighted by the feelings that he was sending to her body.

KB continued to lick her pussy. He felt like he could be in there all day. It tasted real good to him.

"Fuck! I'm cumming!" Thailand moaned, in immense pleasure.

She was trying her best to not moan out loud. KB came up for air and his face was covered in her juices.

"Damn, that shit was so fucking good, mannn!" KB smiled and wiped his face. Her essence was still dripping from his beard, but he didn't care.

Thai was on stuck for a second because that was crazy orgasm she just had. KB picked her up and placed her on the counter. With no words, he unbuckled and unzipped his pants. He pulled Thailand's scrubs and panties all the way off of her body. She had on clogs, so they hit the floor.

"No, Kashim! I'm mad with you." Thai tried to resist what was about to happen.

"This pussy way too wet for you to be blocking. Let me give you this dick." KB looked into her eyes and kneeled down to kiss her.

He pulled his pants and boxers down. Before she knew it, KB entered her with just the head of his dick. They both let out deep moans. Thai was feeling a little pain and he was feeling pleasure.

"Damn, this pussy is crucial as fuck! This shit is mine now. Give my shit away and it's pushing up daisies for that nigga. Shit, I might even kill yo' thick ass." KB groaned out, as he went inside of her, inch by inch.

"Ooohhhhh!" Thai yelped, with her eyes closed and biting her bottom lip.

KB stood, motionless for a second. He knew if he started moving, he would cum. Thai had that super soaker. He had never experienced something so great. He had been with so many women in his twenty-three years, but this was by far the best ever. He couldn't even explain the spark he felt when he entered Thai. She had his mind going blank.

Recovering from his trance, KB started moving his lower body. He was stroking her deep and slow. To keep himself from cumming again, KB pulled out and went back to licking her pussy.

"Oh my damn! Kashim, this is so good!"

"I love the way you say my name. This the best shit a nigga done had!" KB slipped and said as he penetrated her again.

They continued to sex each other. They changed positions and KB entered her from behind. He had to keep his hand over her mouth because he was giving her nothing, but hard and rapid strokes.

"Nurse Reynolds, you are needed in the ICU. Nurse Reynolds, you are needed in the ICU!" Came blaring from the speakers.

Thailand moved up and KB's dick fell out of her with a pop. She broke from his embrace and went to the napkin dispenser, pulled some out and started wetting them with warm water. She cleaned herself up and fixed her hair. She placed her scrubs back on her body and discarded the napkins. KB cleaned his dick and pulled his pants back up.

"I wasn't playing with yo' ass, Thai. What time you get off?"

"I get off at seven." She replied and then headed out of the bathroom.

€€€€€€€

KB stood on the wall and caught his breath. He didn't know what he got himself into. He just took her virginity and honestly, it felt like he would be the one that would go crazy, instead of the other way around.

He left out of the bathroom and took the elevator to go to Burnah's room.

"Where the fuck you been at?" Zip called out to KB.

"I had some shit I needed to handle for a second."

"Well, we have a meeting tomorrow. Make sure you're there." Gallardo announced and walked out of the room, with Gretchen following close behind.

"Ight." KB walked further into the room and saw that Burnah was asleep.

He decided he would spend some time with him and wait for Thai to get off. KB wanted to get back in them guts again.

That girl just don't know how fucked up imma be about that pussy." He thought to himself, with a big smile.

€€€€€€€

The next day, the men sat in this apartment where they conducted business. Gallardo, Burnah, Tress, Zip, and KB were the only ones allowed in there. They didn't trust anyone else in there. They scheduled shipments, held the work, and it served as their safe-house. It was in Beverly Hills and in Gallardo's mother's name.

"Okay, now that we are all here, except for Burnah...let's get this meeting started. So, Zip and KB y'all got some info from Anjee. What did she say?"

"She basically said that the niggas who kicked in the door at the Lynwood spot was Crips and they were getting revenge for Lathan."

"His cousin is a Crip from Crenshaw. I bet it was his ass. Tress, I need you to keep him and his boys under surveillance. I will send you the pic and shit later." Gallardo instructed to him.

"Aight."

"So, what you got planned for these niggas, bruh? You want me to get Beanz and his crew to handle it." Zip was referring to the Bloods that they kept on their payroll.

"Naw, imma handle this when we come back from Colombia. Until then, we just going to watch them niggas and then make our move. Aight, meeting adjourned. I gotta get back to the crib and pack. Aight, Keep them eyes open because them niggas plotting. Have the banga on ya to show em the militia behind ya." He recited their creed.

"Same shit, different day when the militia is behind ya." They all responded, in unison.

The men dapped each other up and left the apartment. KB rode to his house and decided to see what Thai was up to.

KB: WAKE YO ASS UP?

KB: I WANT YOU AT MY CRIB BUTT ASS NAKED.

KB: Oh yeah, cook me a steak and some chicken and shrimp alfredo too.

He placed his phone on his lap and weaved in and out of traffic on the 405 Freeway. He was driving his Maserati this time. He heard his phone chime and picked it up.

THAI: FUCK YOU!

KB: You know Daddy don't like backtalk. Imma handle that pussy. I'll be there in twenty five minutes tops.

KB let out a chuckle and placed his phone in the cup holder. He had to focus now because there was an accident a few feet in front of him. He was blaring California Love through his speakers and bobbing his head. He had a lot of shit on his mind, but Thai was proving to be his stress reliever. He hadn't even known her for a long time and she was already sleeping in his crib. *Was it possible that baby had me sprung, already?* He asked himself, aloud.

Nawwwww! He answered as he lit the pre-rolled joint that was in his other cup holder. Only time would tell if the savage would let anyone in his heart.

10

HEAVY

*R*unning on zero energy, Gallardo was ready to sleep, but that wasn't happening anytime soon. He had just returned from a two-day trip to Colombia to meet with their connect, Enrikqto.. Zip accompanied him to the trip. Both of them were tired, but business came first. They were in the car with two of their most trusty workers, Humble and Serry. They were on their way to the barbershop to make an example out of the dudes that shot Burnah and their young heads, in the Lynwood Spot. They robbed them of the money and product in the trap house. The take was over three hundred large and ten kilos of pure cocaine They weren't able to get the stuff out of Burnah's trunk, but they walked away with a lot. They had a snitch within their crew and he put Gallardo on to what happened. Tress killed the man with his bare hands after he gave them the information that they needed. They would not keep someone that was willing to snitch, alive. There was no hesitation in that. He met the fate that was deserved to him, as far as the Militia was concerned.

Despite not sleeping right, he also was backed up sexually and he had been thinking about Nikayla a lot. Since the shooting at *IHOP*, she'd been playing him to the left. With most girls, he would have said fuck you, but it was something about the pretty-eyed beauty that had his mind gone. He planned to surprise her at work when he finished handling the business at the barbershop. She was a nurse at *University of Central Los Angeles Medical Center.* Per his sister, Gretchen, Gallardo found out that she was working the seven a.m. to seven p.m. shift. She went to lunch at four o' clock, so he planned to be done with everything he needed to do befor heading there. His mind was still on what he planned to do once he surprised her. He had to put that in the back of his mind, so he could focus on the task at hand. This had to be handled. He had to show people that the *Black Mask Militia* was not to be fucked with. They had to get rid of the weak links in the chain before it spreads like a cancer.

"The niggas supposed to be in *Br3w's Barbershop* in Torrance. Tress is sitting outside waiting on us right now," Zip revealed, taking a puff from the Raw paper joint he was smoking.

"Aight, we should be there shortly." Gallardo let it be known as he laid his head on the headrest.

Humble was driving the Chevy Impala that they were utilizing. This was what they called their mission car. They rode around in this blacked out car when they had BHM business to take care of. This occasion was no different than any others.

Five minutes later, they arrived at the barbershop and parked across the street. They all got out of the car in their all black. Gallardo wore a black Polo v-neck, black Levi's, all black Converses and a bandanna around his neck. Tress jumped out of his surveillance car and they walked across the street with their guns already drawn. There was no one hanging out in front of the barbershop, so they didn't have to worry about too many witnesses. The men walked into the barbershop, locked the door behind them and slid the privacy shade down.

"Can I help you, gentlemen?" The owner asked, in a choppy tone.

Gallardo was sure that they noticed the guns in their hands.

"You can't, but they can." Gallardo pointed to the dudes that were said to have ran up on Burnah and their workers.

"I don't know about that, Youngblood. I don't know what business you have with my son, but my establishment is not where you handle that."

"Naw, old head, you don't understand." Gallardo didn't care for the peaceful approach that this man was trying to be on. It was beyond that point. Now, it was time to kill.

"Naw, I don't think you understand. Get the fuck out of my daddy's shop! You should've thought about that shit 'fore you killed Doon. Fuck you!" The man's son stood up and pulled his gun out.

His crew tried to join in, but Zip, Humble, and Serry shot them all, straight headshots. The patrons in the shop were all horrified by the scene before them.

"Does this make you understand where I'm coming from?" Gallardo laughed and showed the gold and diamonds at the top and bottom of his teeth. He had these beautiful brown eyes, but they were black in this moment.

"I don't give a f—," Zip pulled the trigger on him, emptying the whole clip before he could say anything else.

His father cried over his son's body, but they didn't care at all. They came in there and served their purpose.

"Serry, call the cleaning crew. We are going to stay here until they come through. Which one of y'all wanna cut my hair?" Gallardo asked, with a smile on his face.

He was acting like it was normal for someone to cut his hair, with four bodies laying on the ground, lifeless. Gallardo didn't care about that at all.

€€€€€€€

After dealing with what happened at the barbershop and going home to shower, Gallardo went to *Naab Café* to get Nikayla's favorites. She loved Mediterranean food and he was going to make that happen for her. Once he picked up the foods she liked, Gallardo made his way to this florist named Ferimo, who his father always went to when he was giving his mother and wife flowers. Mr. Ferimo owned a shop called *In Full Bloom* on Pico Boulevard, near the *Santa Monica Pier*.

Being that it was a Wednesday afternoon, the shop wasn't as full as it was on the weekend. In another life, Gallardo could see himself being a horticulturist in a flower shop. Too bad that wasn't the cards he was dealt in this game called life. The smell of flowers calmed him and the made him just reflect on life.

"I see that you're back, Gallardo." Mr. Ferimo greeted him, with a handshake.

"Yes, sir. You know that ya flowers are the truth." He complimented the old man.

Mr. Ferimo put you in the mindset of Mario from the Nintendo video game. He was short Italian man with a thick mustache and thinning hair on his head. He wore Brut and kept his hair slick and greasy. Typical Italian in the way that he dressed.

"Am I making you the usual arrangements for ya sisters and mother?"

"Yes, I will take those to be sent to them, but I also have another request." Gallardo announced, with more of a smile on his face than he intended.

"Yes, yes, I can fulfill any request that you make, Mr. Miller. Looks like you like this girl. I know that face because it was the one I gave my wife when I was courting her in the 70s." Mr. Ferimo divulged to Gallardo.

"I need something that shows that I really like her and I'm looking forward to seeing where things go."

"I have just the thing for you! Follow me." Mr. Ferimo exclaimed, excitedly.

For a heavyset man, he moved pretty fast and seemed to be full of energy. They made it over to his extensive garden and stopped in front of the yellow roses, but these looked different because they had red tips.

"What's with the red tips?" Gallardo looked over at him, confusingly.

"These particular roses mean friendship or falling in love. Three of these mean love at first sight." Mr. Ferimo explained, as he grabbed his gardening gloves and the special shears he used to cut the flowers.

"Just give me a dozen of them and we are good.

Once Gallardo paid for all of his items, he was now on the way to see Nikayla. Staring at his watch as he sat in traffic, he had like twenty minutes before she went to lunch. Taking his phone out, he decided to text Nikayla and see what she was up to.

Gallardo: Aye, beautiful...u have been a hard person to get ahold of.
Nikayla: About to go on my lunch break. Been busy with school, work, and my son.

GALLARDO: UNDERSTANDABLE

NIKAYLA: I WILL TEXT YOU WHEN I GO ON BREAK. I HAVE TO
FINISH UP WITH THIS PATIENT.

Gallardo: Aight.

He placed his phone down and traffic was finally moving so that he
could make it to the hospital where Nikayla worked.

€€€€€€€

Gallardo walked into the building and took the elevator to the
Women's Center section where she worked. He walked to the nurses'
station to find her. He was a little nervous because he saw India, who
happened to be Mia's sister.

"Hey, how may I help you?" She tried to play it off like she didn't
know him and Gallardo was sure that she noticed the roses in his
hand in the big ass vase.

"I'm here to see Nikayla. Is she still here?"

"One second." India got on the phone and paged Nikayla to come
to the nurses' station.

"She should be up here, shortly. So, are you still messing with my
sister?" India pried into his business.

"I mean...me and ya sister had an arrangement, but I plan on dropping things soon. Not that it's really any of ya business...I happen to like Nikayla."

"I'm asking because I don't want to see my friend get hurt or my sister."

"You don't have to worry about that." Gallardo replied, hoping that Nikayla would hurry up and make it to the nurses' station.

He also hoped that India didn't make a big deal out of this. She was known to be messy and he knew she was going to run back to Mia and let her know about this.

Nikayla walked up to the nurses' station and noticed Gallardo standing there. She smiled because even after all of the busy days and nights, he still seemed interested.

"Hey, you! Why didn't you tell me you were coming up here when we were texting earlier?"

"I wanted to surprise you with lunch and these." Gallardo motioned toward the food in his hand and the roses.

"Ohmigosh, these are beautiful. Let me go place these in the office and then we can go to the cafeteria," Nikayla walked to the back of the nurses' station and headed through a door.

India was texting away on her phone, so he knew that she was probably telling her sister. He let out a deep sigh and rolled his eyes upward. This messy bitch don't have anything else better to do with her life.

"Okay, I'm back." Nikayla returned and they headed to the elevator, so they could take it down to the lobby. The cafeteria was on the first floor.

They stood on the elevator with other people, in a comfortable silence. Gallardo's phone was vibrating on his hip, but he wasn't concerned about it. Nikayla would have all of his time. Once they exited the elevator, they walked into the cafeteria.

"You want something to drink?" Gallardo asked her, as they stood in line.

"Sure. I'll take a bottle of cranberry juice."

"Aight, go find us a seat."

Nikayla walked off and left him to get the drinks.

€€€€€€€

"Wheeewww, I'm stuffed," Nikayla rubbed her stomach as she spoke.

"That shit was actually kinda good. Never fucked with Mediterranean food before today."

"Well, you don't know what you missing. I'm half Middle Eastern and this is the food I grew up on." Nikayla confided in him.

"Man, what color are yo' eyes?" I swear them bitches are beautiful." Gallardo complimented as he stared at her.

"You're one to talk. Yas are beautiful as well."

"Naw, love. That sound gay as fuck. My eyes just look nice." Gallardo scrunched his face up and couldn't help, but laugh.

"Okay, you're right. I have to get back to work, but I had a nice time talking with you and eating lunch." Nikayla stood up and stretched a little.

There were doctors, nurses, families, and other employees meandering around the cafeteria, not paying them any mind.

"Aight. Text me when you get off. Might pull up on you tonight."

"Okay, just let me know." Nikayla gave him a hug and they went their separate ways.

Gallardo had never felt for a girl like this before. He hoped that it lasted and Nikayla didn't try to play him. He wouldn't hesitate to kill her. Women failed to realize that men are capable of being fully invested and will not hesitate to pull a trigger when it comes to affairs of their heart.

Now that Gallardo was finished with hanging with his future wife, he pulled out his phone to check his messages. He had a few from Mia and two from his young head, Humble.

Mia: So, you fucking bitches that work with my sister?

MIA: WHY AREN'T YOU RESPONDING?

MIA: DOES THIS MEAN THAT I CAN'T GET ANY MORE OF
THAT BIG DICK?

Mia: Heavy, how you going to play me? You made promises.

Gallardo had to keep himself from laughing at the messages he just read. Mia and her sister were crazy as hell. He knew that India's messy ass was going to tell her sister about seeing him. She was mostly salty because Gallardo wouldn't fuck her. All she did was suck his dick on a drunken night. Mia didn't even know about that and he was sure that she would fuck her sister up if she found out. Still feeling tickled, he opened up Humble's message.

Humble: Serry and I found them other niggas in Long Beach. They banging and around a bunch of them crab ass niggas.

GALLARDO: I'M ON THE WAY

Gallardo hopped in his truck and headed to Long Beach. That was Crip territory mostly, but Gallardo didn't give a fuck. He was the type that would stand in the middle of a Crip block with a red bandanna on his mouth and dare any of the niggas to come out on some dumb shit. Most people let the pretty and alluring eyes fool them. Gallardo was a ticking time bomb just waiting to happen.

11

NIKAYLA

"*W*hy you smiling so hard?" Nikayla's co-worker, India asked, being nosy as hell.

Nikayla rolled her eyes, upward and counted to five in her head. She couldn't stand India because she was messy and tried to find any subject she could to be the hospital's gossip. They used to be good friends, until Nikayla saw her true colors. The only thing that kept her from beating India's ass was the fact that she had a job and reputation to uphold. Other than that, she would've been fucked her up.

"Nothing much. Just high off life to be honest."

"Well, I hope it wasn't because of Heavy. I mean, he is fucking my sister. I just thought I would warn you. He isn't who he claims to be."

"Duly noted, India. I will keep that in mind. I have to get back to work." Nikayla laughed, inwardly.

India was always trying to throw salt at her. She found it funny that she would tell her that Gallardo was fucking her sister. She really didn't care because it wasn't like they were in a relationship or anything. All they did was have a nice, stimulating conversation and lunch together.

After work, Nikayla went to go pick Naheem up from Nathan's mother's house. Though Nathan was dead, Nikayla did not keep her son away from his father's family. They were very much a pivotal part of his life. The only person she didn't deal with was Nathan's brother, Nehemiah. Nehemiah was crazy and she didn't even want her son to associate with him. Nehemiah was one of the leaders of the *Nutty Blocc Compton Crips* and a livewire. Nikayla couldn't stand him mainly because he was the reason why Nathan did a lot of things that he did. The bank robbery that resulted from his demise was his initiation into the gang. When she found out, Nikayla was pissed, but she couldn't be too mad because Nathan was a grown man and there was no gun to his head or anything that said he "had" to rob the bank and participate in a police chase with *LAPD*. He chose to do those things with the notion that he would be gang-affiliated.

Nikayla knocked on Ms. Wanda's door and waited for her to come open it. She stood there looking at her phone as she waited. A few seconds later, she heard the screen door and the door with burglar bars open. Looking up, she met the chest of Nehemiah. He was standing there eyeing her like she was a piece of meat. Nikayla rolled her eyes and cleared her throat.

"Wassup, Nik Nik? Looking sexy as fuck." He licked his lips and showed her his bad teeth that were covered by gold and diamond grills.

She wouldn't be surprised if it was cubic zirconium in his mouth. Nehemiah really wasn't out here making money like that. He was always in and out of jail and still living in his mother's house.

"Are Ms. Wanda and Naheem here?" Nikayla asked, annoyed with his presence.

"Naw, they went to the store. Come in and sit down."

"No, I'm good...I'll wait in my car." Nikayla made her way down the steps to head to the driveway.

"You think you too good for me because you a nurse and shit. You still a bum bitch." Nehemiah barked, mad that she rejected him.

"Whatever." Nikayla gave him her back and opened her doors, so she could wait for her son.

She couldn't stand Nehemiah and couldn't see why women even liked him. He was a disrespectful nigga.

€€€€€€€

Later that night, Nikayla sat on the couch studying for a test she had for class. It was midnight and Naheem was in his room calling the hogs. That was her perfect time to study— when he was sleeping. As she was getting up to grab some water, she heard the front door opening, slowly. Gretchen was trying to sneak in the house. Her shoes were in her hands, along with her purse and cellphone.

"Well, well, well, I didn't think you stayed her anymore." Nikayla remarked, sarcastically.

"Hey, sis. Wasn't trying to wake you." Gretchen smiled, nervously.

"Girllll! I'm sitting up here studying for this test. I was already up. Why you coming all in here late night creeping?"

"I was with Tress."

"I know that. So, are y'all fucking now? Bitch I want details!" Nik Nik perked up and was being nosy.

"There's nothing really do tell. All we do is go out to eat, hang out at his house, and study. Nothing else."

"I don't think I could be in the bed with a man that looks like Tress and just sleep. How do you do it?"

"I don't knowwww! All I know is that it's hard as hell. Tress is so motherfucking fine and he's so sweet." GG whined, with a smile on her face.

"I'm glad that y'all are finally taking that next step. I know you are the one who told Gallardo what time I go on break."

"Yes, I did, hoe. I know you want my brother and he want you too."

"Can I be truthful with you, sis?" Nikayla looked at Gretchen, with a serious expression on her face.

"Yeah, of course."

"I really like Gallardo, but I don't know if I'm ready to be with someone with a lifestyle like his. A kingpin only has two places they can go, either jail or the morgue. You see what happened with Nathan."

"I know that this is hard on you, but you have to take a leap of faith. It's been almost three years since Nathan...I'm not saying jump into something, but you deserve to be happy and live life. All you do is go to school, work, and take care of my godbaby. You gotta live a little."

"I hear ya." Nikayla went back to studying and GG went to her room.

She left Nikayla with something to think about. She wanted to be with Gallardo, but had a gut feeling that things would go left.

Let's hope that this doesn't backfire in my face. She mused to herself, with a deep sigh.

*L*eaving Tress was the last thing that she wanted to do, but she had to sleep in her own bed. Gretchen also didn't want him to get tired of her. Their relationship was still fresh and new. That night at *Wolfgang Puck Express*, they decided to make it official. Since that night, GG had been staying at Tress' house. They would go to class, eat dinner, watch Netflix, and work out in his home gym. They were binge watching *Grey's Anatomy*, since neither one of them had seen it. They had yet to have sex. All they did was heavy kiss and dry hump. Both of them wanted to continue getting to know one another before they took it there.

As she sat on her bed, she couldn't help, but reach for her phone and text him.

GG: I miss you already. Is that crazy?
Tress: No. I miss ya little ass too. I honestly don't know how imma sleep tonight.

GG: AWWWW

TRESS: I WANNA COME PICK YOU UP AFTER I GET DONE WITH
THIS BUSINESS I GOTTA HANDLE WITH YA BROTHER.

GG: You know where the spare key is. You can just stay the night.
Tress: It will be late as fuck, but I will be coming through.

GG: I HOPE SO

She placed her phone on her bed and went to take a bath. She just wanted to place one of her bath bombs in the tub and relaxed. She knew she would probably be sleep when Tress came in, but she was going to make sure she was ready in case things got hot and heavy between them. It had been a long time since her queen size bed had any action.

TRESS

*W*hen Gallardo called him and told him that they had some business to handle, he had to drop GG off at home. He didn't want her to leave his sight, but she decided to go home since she hadn't been there in about a week. He loved her company and she helped him fall asleep better. Most nights, he was basically up worried about his family and wondering why she did the things that she did.

Tress arrived at the address that Gallardo gave him in Long Beach. He was told to bring his tools and to come alone. Tress was dressed in a black tank top, black joggers, and his standard black Timberland boots. Though he wasn't from up North, he kept a pair of Timbs for missions. He jumped out of the Impala they used for missions and threw the black bandanna on his mouth. Gallardo was standing outside, in the dark waiting for Tress. Tress walked over to where he was.

"Ay, bruh, what's going on? You ain't sound too good on the phone."

"Shit went a lil left, my nigga. I knew that I could only call you to deal with this." Gallardo walked to the back of the house they were at and both of them walked through the door. He led Tress to the crime scene he left there. There were two bodies on the floor, lifeless. There was blood pooling under them both.

"Damn, what happened?"

"Humble and Serry called me and let me know that the rest of the niggas who ran up on Burnah and the young heads was out here in LBC. I waited until they were away from their crew and ran up in this spot."

"I got this...you just head on out." Tress informed him, removing the black bandanna from his mouth.

"Naw, I feel that I need to help you get this shit cleaned up."

"This is my job, bruh. Imma call the little nigga, Allure and have him help me with this. His ass in training anyway."

"Aight, Keep them eyes open because them niggas plotting. Have the banga on ya to show em the militia behind ya."

"Same shit, different day when the Militia behind ya." Tress responded, to the creed they all lived by.

Gallardo dapped him up and left out of the back door. Tress pulled out his phone from his back pocket. He called his protege, Allure. Allure answered on the third ring. It sounded like he was in the middle of fucking someone.

"Hello! Who the fuck is this...shit, girl this pussy is fire!"

"Ay, lil nigga...get out of the pussy. I need you to meet me somewhere...my car is broke down and I got two flat tires. Bring yo' tool kit." Tress was speaking in code.

That was their code for bodies. They knew it was better to not say too much over the phones. You never knew who was listening.

"Shittttt!" Allure yelled out, in frustration.

"That pussy must be real good." Tress chuckled, in amusement.

"Fuck you, bruh. Email me the addy and I'll be there." Allure hung up the phone and Tress placed his phone back in his pocket.

The air was filled with the metallic smell of blood. Tress sat on the edge of the sofa and waited for Allure to show up. His job was bloody and demanding, but he took pride in helping his boys in any way possible. He had to hurry and get this job finished as fast as possible. They were deep in Crip gang territory.

€€€€€€€

"Aight, we are done now. Thanks for coming through for me, youngen." Tress dapped Allure up.

They had finally finished cutting up the bodies with a saw and placed them in heavy duty tarps and garbage cans. The place was spotless after they cleaned up all of the blood and brain matter that Gallardo left in his wake.

"No need to thank me. I live for this shit here. It gives me this rush." Allure responded, lighting the pre-rolled joint he had behind his ear.

"You jumped out the pussy quick and got here fast as fuck."

"That hoe had some good shit on her. Believe it or not, I was down the street. Some lil bitch I met out at *Fox Hills Mall* had me in the crib while her husband was out of town on business." Allure replied, taking a pull of his joint.

"Damn." Tress doubled over, in laughter.

"Shit was crazy. I didn't know she was married until I was in the crib. Bitch live in this nice ass house and her nigga a doctor."

"Baby girl said the good doctor wasn't hitting her right, huh?" Tress poked fun at Allure.

"I guess so. She let that nose candy get in her system and bob on my dick like some carnival apples. Doc sniff that shit, too. That's where the bitch get the habit from. Enough about my shit though...now that this shit is done, you can head to yo' crib, I'll dispose of this shit."

"Gotcha. Aight, Keep them eyes open because them niggas plotting. Have the banga on ya to show em the militia behind ya."

"Same shit, different day, when the Militia behind ya." Allure picked up the garbage bags and his tool kit and they left out of the back door. Once Allure had everything squared away in his mission truck, they went their separate ways.

€€€€€€€

Tress got on the freeway to go pick GG up. It wasn't too many cars on the road so it wasn't going to take him too long to get to her. He pulled out his iPhone so that he could text her to be ready.

TRESS: YOU STILL UP?

GG: YES.

Tress: Aight. I'm about to pull up in a few. Be waiting for me.
GG: Okay.
Tress: See you in a few.

He raced through the freeway and was anxious to pick up his lady. He really liked Gretchen and she was proving to be his peace in this cold world. Only time would tell if she remained that way. He just hoped that she did.

€€€€€€€

The next day, Tress and Gretchen were in the gym getting their daily workout in. Tres couldn't help, but stare at the sweat as it dripped from her smooth, chocolaty skin. All he wanted to do was fuck the shit out of her. That's been on his mind for a long time. His thoughts were intensifying as he stared at her body. His manhood was hardening in response to him ogling her body.

Gretchen removed her headphones and looked over at Tress. She noticed that he was in a trance. His eyes were intensely staring at her. She felt the heat radiating from his body. She was sure that he could feel the heat coming off of her too. The sexual tension in the room was almost deafening. It was so thick that both of them couldn't even talk. Gretchen walked over to the treadmill that Tress was standing on and stood in front of him. He leaned down and their lips met. Tress picked her up and she instantly wrapped her legs around his waist. He held her by the back of her calves and their kiss deepened to their tongues dancing a sensual tango.

"Take all of this shit off. NOW!" Tress demanded, his voice booming in his home gym.

He let GG down from their embrace and she obliged his request. Tress removed his gym shorts and boxers. He kept on his Nike running shoes. Gretchen stood in front of him, fully naked. Tress picked her back up, but this time, he wrapped her legs around his neck. Gretchen was a little scared that he would drop her. She voiced that, but he quickly eased her mind.

"I don't lift weights for nothing...I'm not going to drop you." Tress assured her as he locked her legs in hands. He had turned the treadmill on and it was moving under his feet.

As soon as she was secured, he instructed her to ride his tongue as he ran on the treadmill. It was something he always wanted to do and now he finally had a willing and able victim to play "Fuck 'n Fitness" with. This had been a fantasy for him and he was finally fulfilling it.

Gretchen tasted good against his tongue. Tress didn't want to stop licking up her juices. He would make sure that she knew just how it felt to get head from a savage. Gretchen just didn't know what was in store for her. Her pussy was his obstacle course and he planned to show her just what she had been missing.

"Oh, my FUCK!" GG screamed out, in ecstasy.

Keep screaming, that shit excite a nigga like me. Tress thought, as he continued to lick her to oblivion. She had nowhere to go and would definitely get a workout, fucking with him.

14

THAILAND

*A*fter the whole hospital incident, Thai made sure that she avoided KB in any way that she could. He was batshit crazy to her and she couldn't deal at times. She had to admit that the sex in the bathroom was awesome. It wasn't the ideal place to lose ya virginity, but Thai knew that KB wasn't a conventional man. He was rough, rude, and sexy as hell. Standing at 6'2, with his milk chocolate skin, thin, muscular build, dark bedroom eyes, unruly hair and beard, KB was the total package and she was sure that he got around, like that Tupac song. He reminded her of him as well. They favored each other a little.

As she sat in her living room on her off day, she heard a knock on her door. She found that to be odd because no one really knew where she stayed and she didn't socialize with anyone who lived in the apartments. There was no reason for her to, to be honest. She placed the nail brush back into the glass of polish and hobbled over to the door, careful not to mess up her toenails. She was lounging in the front of her house, painting her toes in a mauve color. She had her favorite snacks on the table and was tuned into Blackish, which happened to be one of her favorite shoes these days. She was streaming it on Hulu. Thai gazed through her peephole and saw that it was KB standing there with bags in his hands. She swung the door open and gave him major attitude.

"Why are you here, Kashim?" Her arms were crossed along her chest and she had a scowl on her face.

"A nigga came to check on yo' stubborn ass and shit. Now, move!" He pushed the door open and kind of forced her to let him in.

"Gee, Kashim...why don't you just come in?" Sarcasm oozed from her voice and he just found it funny as hell.

"Damn, the queen pin ain't teach you no manners?" That's what he called Thailand's mother, Tandy since she didn't like to speak of her.

Thai was still a little salty about her parents cutting off, but it would be a cold day in hell before she begged them for any of it back.

"Fuck the Queen pin. I make my own rules." Thai rolled her eyes and walked to her living room.

"So, you gonna keep ignoring a nigga?" KB got straight to the point.

"What do you want from me, Kashim? You were the one that said you didn't fuck with virgins. I'm confused because you were the one who fucked me at the hospital."

"I know what I said. For some reason, I can't leave yo' stuck up ass alone. That shit is pissing me off, so I guess imma just have to go with the flow." KB revealed to her, candidly.

"Well, I'm not trying to be ya test subject for a twisted ass relationship." Thai scrunched her face up at him.

"A nigga ain't say shit about a relationship. I'm trying to take you out so we can grub and chill."

"I don't want to go anywhere with you."

"Why not?"

"I don't think that you know it, but ya ass is crazy. I can't deal with that." Thai kept it real with him.

"What that got to do with anything? Crazy niggas need love too." KB was dead serious with what he said to her.

"Kashim, can you just leave? I don't feel like dealing with the back and forth with you." Thai sighed, exasperated with the whole banter between herself and KB.

"Just let me take you out and I will leave you alone," KB put on his charming smile, hoping it would win her over.

"Ughhhhh, okay! One date and if you ruin it, then that's it. There's no coming back from that."

"Aight, I gotcha. I'll be back to pick you up at eight." KB announced, while looking down at his watch.

"Yeah, whatever." Thai rolled her eyes at him, in annoyance.

"That rolling of the eyes shit is ratchet as fuck. Chill with all of that before I put this big dick in yo' life." KB grabbed his dick, for emphasis.

"See, you just had to mess up the moment. Can you get out, so that I can take a nap? Work was kind of trying last night." Thai let out a yawn.

"Aight, I'm out. Imma come through later, though. Wear some sexy shit for me. Something where I could easily pull yo' panties to the side or don't wear any panties at all. Either way would suit me." KB placed a kiss on her neck and Thai moved away before he could try anything else.

KB walked out of the door and she slammed it in his face before he could say anything else.

"Damn, yo' little ass is cold as hell. You got that though, ma." KB laughed out loud and Thai rolled her eyes, in irritation on the other side of the door.

Thai went to her room to go take her nap. She was too tired to do anything else.

After her nap, Thai woke up and went in her closet to see what she would be wearing that night. She honestly was nervous about going out with KB. He was crazy as hell, but he set her body on fire. Since the night that he "bust her cherry," his words, not hers, she had been fantasizing and thinking about him. KB had a big ass dick and despite the pain, the pleasure was rewarding. If he played his cards right, they could be fucking for the rest of the night.

€€€€€€€

After much searching, Thai decided on this black two piece Givenchy crop top and skirt set, a pair of rose gold Giuseppe Zanotti stiletto heels, and rose gold accessories. She took her braids and placed them in a bun. She did her own hair since she knew no one in LA or Compton, for that matter. Once she was finished with getting dressed, she sprayed pumps of Oscar de La Renta Extraordinary perfume in the designated spots of her body.

"Damn, you fine as fuck." KB announced, as soon as Thailand opened the door and came into his view.

"You look nice, Kashim." She complimented him, with a smile.

KB cleaned up pretty nice. He was wearing a crisp white dress shirt, a black velvet blazer, black fitted slacks, and some black and white dress shoes.

"You ready?" He asked, looking at her for confirmation.

"Yeah. Let me just lock up." Thai ushered him out of the apartment and locked the door.

They walked outside and KB's Range Rover was parked all crooked. He didn't care, so she wasn't going to address it.

"How many cars do you have?"

"Four. I barely drive this shit, so I wanted you to keep it. That raggedy ass car you drive now ain't cool." KB remarked, leaving out of the parking lot of her building.

"I can't take this car...no." Thai resisted, though she really could see herself driving it.

"Wasn't up for discussion." KB replied, ending the conversation between them.

"Whatever." Thai mumbled and rolled her eyes at him.

€€€€€€€

After a little bit of driving, they arrived at *Providence* seafood restaurant on Melrose. Thai was lowkey excited to taste their food.

She hadn't been to a fancy restaurant since she left Philly a few months back.

"I usually don't come to restaurants like this, but I know this shit you used to do with kingpin and queenpin though." KB decreed, flatly.

"Kashim, you didn't have to bring me here to prove something. I would be cool with just a regular restaurant." Thai iterated to him, with a frown.

"Ain't this the bullshit you used to?"

"Used to and what I actually do are two different things."

"Aight. Let's just go in and eat. A nigga hungry as fuck. Stomach touching my back."

"Let's go." Thai replied and he gave her a peck on the lips.

They got out of the truck and a valet guy came over to grab the keys from KB.

"Look here, lil nigga. Don't fuck up her shit...I'll have yo' ass dead swimming in the LA River, if you catch my drift. Don't fuck with me." KB threatened, scaring the hell out of the valet.

"Yes...yes, sir." The young man stuttered, as he grasped the keys in his hand.

They headed into the restaurant to the hostess desk.

"Was all of that even necessary?"

"Hell yeah." KB responded, in his typical nonchalant manner.

After KB told the hostess who he was, she started directing them to their table. As they were being seated, there was an old man wearing sunglasses just standing there. Thai could see the anger in KB's eyes as he approached the man. She felt so embarrassed in that moment.

"Ay, bruh, stop staring at my bitch! Just because you got them dark ass sunglasses on don't mean I ain't peep yo pervertic ass looking. That's all my ass back there!"

"Look here, young man. I'm—," before he could finish his sentence, KB hauled off and punched him in the mouth, twice.

The man hit the floor with a loud thud. The restaurant became so quiet that it was deafening. All eyes were on KB, the man on the ground, and Thailand. Her mouth was open so wide that a bee could've stung her right on the tongue. She was so shocked KB had punched this old man in the face. The quietness was soon replaced with gasps and someone running over to the scene.

"Ohmigosh! You hit my grandfather! He's blind!" The lady yelled, frantically as she rushed to help him up.

"Shit. My bad." KB apologized in his own way.

"I should have your ass arrested." The lady scoffed, in disgust.

"Bitch, I apologized. Move the hell on with that bullshit." KB spat, directing his attention to the lady.

Thai found her bearings and ran out of the restaurant. KB didn't follow her. He knew she was mad, so he let her take the Range Rover and called Humble to pick him up, since he was an Uber driver.

I gotta stay away from that crazy motherfucker! Thai mused to herself, as she waited for the valet to bring the Range Rover to the front of the restaurant.

15

BURNAH

"*A*rgghhh!! Fucckkkk!" Burnah hollered out, in serious pain. He tried to stretch and was given the reminder of why he was in the hospital in the first place. He was shot five times, but blessed to still be alive and just recovering. The only thing that was a problem was his hip. He found out he had to have physical therapy and walk with a cane. He was pissed at first, but the solace he got in knowing that Lathan and his crew was pushing up daisies, was worth it all. In this past week, he hadn't seen Gina and she wasn't returning his calls or texts. He knew she was in town because Gallardo and GG mentioned it when they came to see him the other day. He felt some type of way that she hadn't been there to see him. They were beefing right now, but he felt like she could dead the dumb shit and come see him.

Just when he was about to call the nurse, someone walked in the room. He looked up and saw that it was Gina. She walked further in the room and sat down. Just by her body language, Burnah could tell that she was still very much upset about what transpired between them. He just wanted her to get over the shit already. She usually did.

"I'm only here because you got shot and gonna need to help." Gina was extremely cold and rigid.

"So, you gonna be a cold bitch to me?" Burnah was getting aggravated.

"You lucky I'm even here, so ya best bet is to just sit there and leave me the hell alone."

"Munchie, just because a nigga down, don't forget who the fuck ya are talking to!" Burnah's voice boomed in the hospital room.

"I'm well aware of who I'm talking to, Briggan. You think I give a fuck?" She stared at him and waited for his answer.

She was the only one that called him by his government as well.

"I honestly don't understand why you are so pissed. You knew what it was when we started this thing last year. I'm not with that settling down shit. Never have been and never will be! That shit is dumb as fuck. Y'all women too emotional for a nigga. All I need is the pussy and the head. That's what makes the world go around." Burnah answered her, in his own little way.

"You sat in my bed and ya bed and made promises. You ain't shit and you know it. For now on, shit will be strictly blasé blasé with us. I'm sick of this back and forth. I'll just find me a nigga that will be all for me. I won't hold you back from ya hoe activities." Gina had tears in her eyes, but refused to let them fall.

That made Burnah feel a little bad, but he didn't know the first thing about comforting someone or trying to love someone. Everything he ever loved abandoned him and he wouldn't give Munchie the chance to do the same. He loved her, but couldn't bring himself to show it. That's just who he was and he made no apologies are justifications about it.

"Try that shit if you want to and that nigga will be floating in the LA River. Don't fuck with me, Munchie! Homie gonna die and I put that on the set. " Burnah snipped and the pain started shooting through his body.

Gina noticed his discomfort and pressed the call button on the remote he was given.

"You can't control me. It's not like you want me. Stop trying to dictate what I do."

"When you let me be the first one in that pussy, I staked owner-ship. Now, don't play with me."

"You're fucking unbelieveable! I'm gone. I'll be back." Gina roughly grasped her purse and walked out of the hospital door.

"MUNCHIE! MUNCHIE, GET YA ASS BACK HERE! STOP ACTING FUCKING STUPID, YO!" Burnah hollered, but his demand fell on deaf ears.

Gina was gone and there was no telling if she was really coming back. The nurse came in and gave him medicine for the pain and something to relax him as well. Before he knew it, he was succumbing to a deep sleep.

€€€€€€€

Waking up from his sleep, he saw that Zip, Humble, and Serry were playing dice in the corner of the room. He couldn't help, but crack up. These niggas took the hood everywhere that they went. They didn't care at all.

"Seven, niggas! Run me my gwap!" Humble called out, bending his tall ass down to collect his winnings.

"Naw, bet that shit back up." Serry was terrible at shooting dice, but kept playing all the time.

"Y'all some ignant ass niggas, loc. All in my room playing craps and shit."

"Damn, I thought ya bitch ass was in a coma." Serry young ass clowned Burnah.

"Fuck you. Them drugs they giving a nigga be having me out like a motherfucker." Burnah yawned, still feeling tired from the nap he just had.

"Yo ass need to stay up so one of them sexy ass nurses can come in here. It's a bad ass one I want to drop this dick all up in. Baby got a wedding or engagement ring on, but fuck that. Them be the main ones who be freaky. Their husbands don't know how to fuck 'em right. Can tell by her attitude that she need a deep pipin'!" Serry blurbed out, causing all of them to laugh.

"Shit!" Burnah yelped, the pain meds were wearing off and it hurt to laugh.

"Aye, you good over there my nigga?" Zip asked, his face full of concern.

"This pain in my hip ain't no joke. My head is banging too."

"Let me get one of them nurses to come in here and take care of my boy."

"Appreciate it, bruh." Burnah laid back and closed his eyes.

A few seconds later, he heard the nurse talking, so he opened his eyes. She was a beautiful woman, but she was no Gina. Burnah was missing Munchie and it was pissing him off that she couldn't just wait for him to get all of the fucking on the side out of his system. Sure there wasn't a guarantee that he would change, but she knew how he felt about her. He had a fucked up way of showing it, but Gina had to know that his feelings ran deep. She was the only girl that had a key to all three of his houses, he bought her anything that her heart desired, he bought the Audi that she was pushing, and paid for her miscellaneous things in Texas. She lied to Gallardo and told him that she had a job. She had a small job tutoring children, but it didn't pay as much as she spent. Burnah basically supported her, but he couldn't wane the urge for him to fuck other females. It was just something he did to pass time. He wasn't ready to settle down and would not conform or adapt because Gina wanted him to.

The nurse walked in the room. Serry was standing behind her, where the window was.

"Hey, Mr. Hartsfield, you need something?" She asked, looking at Burnah like she wanted to fuck him.

"Yeah...pain meds, ma. This fucking hip is killing me."

"Sure thing. I will place the order in and be back to administer them to you."

"Okay, cool."

Serry was gesturing behind her as if he was giving her backshots. It took all the men in the room everything not to laugh. The nurse had no idea what he was doing behind her back.

"I'll be right back." She walked out of the room and their eyes were glued to her ass.

Once she was out of the room, they all let out a boisterous fit of laughter.

"Nigga, you a fool!" Zip surmised, shaking his head.

"Did y'all see the ass on baby? I'll fuck the shit out of her. That cameltoe was sitting up pretty in them scrubs. Yo, Burnah, I would have that bitch screaming louder than that hoe in *Freddy vs. Jason*." Serry blurted out, causing all of the men in the room to burst out in laughter.

"Bruh, ya ass is a straight fool, my nigga." Humble replied, sitting against the air conditioner unit that was situated by the window.

"Man, I'm serious. Baby could get this nine, on me."

The men parlayed with Burnah for a little while longer and then left because they had business to handle for the Militia.

€€€€€€€

Burnah was alone in the room and when he texted Gina, she claimed she wasn't returning until the morning. He was watching old reruns of *Friends*. He never watched the show, but it was actually pretty funny. As he was deep in one episode, the sexy nurse from earlier walked into the room. She walked up to Burnah's bed and removed the cover from his body. He only had on a hospital gown because he had to keep his hip wound clear of anything except the gauze.

"What you trying to do?" He inquired, giving her a curious look.

"I seen the way you were looking at me. I want some dick." She stated, boldly.

"I can't really fuck right now, due to the pain in my hip, but you can suck my dick."

"Okay." She smiled and pulled the bottom of the gown up.

Burnah's dick was standing at attention and the nurse licked her lips, in excitement. She stroked his long, thick tool with her hands and started licking the tip.

"Damn," Burnah called out, softly.

The nurse started bobbing up and down on his dick, making Burnah's eyes close. She was giving him some fire head and he wasn't sure how long he would last. Head was one of his weaknesses.

"You like that, baby?" She looked up into his eyes.

"Yeah, but chill with that baby shit. Bob that mouth on this dick and shut the fuck up."

"Yes, daddy." The nurse went back to what she was doing.

Just before Burnah felt his nut building up, he heard a loud gasp. He looked up and Gina was standing there with a bag of *Sr. Cliff's Texas Style Burritos* and drinks in a carrier.

Burnah tried to move the girl's head from in between his lap, but the damage was already done. Gina's first impulse had her throwing the food and drinks at both of them. The tears were coming from eyes as she stood there and contemplated what she was going to say or do next. With no words, she closed the door and ran away from the room as fast as she could.

"Fuccckkkk!" Burnah hit his fists against the hospital bed.

He knew that Gina wouldn't want anything to do with him now. He could tell from the expression on her face.

€€€€€€€

Being out of the hospital and in the house wasn't doing anything, but making Burnah stir crazy. The fact that he couldn't speak to or see Gina had him pissed and sad. He knew he brought this on himself, but he didn't think she would react like this. This wasn't the first time that she caught him sleeping with other girls. She knew what type of nigga he was. Burnah loved Gina, but he was young and rich. Too much pussy was thrown at him and he felt he would be a damn fool or soft as hell if he didn't catch it. He felt that he was too young to be tied down to one girl and wasn't even going to try it. He felt like Gina would be his wife one day if he even decided to settle down.

"Man, what the fuck!" Burnah threw his phone on the bed, in deep frustration.

Gina hadn't answered another call. He was trying to figure out why she was going so hard. She let him slide with most of the shit he did and now she wants to act like he's the Devil or something. She was nowhere to be found when he needed her the most.

Zip and KB came over to keep him company and Burnah could barely concentrate from the pills he was taking and the fact that he was lowkey incensed with and missed Gina. His Munchie kept him calm and he enjoyed her being under him. It felt like he was naked out here and lost his soulmate. He couldn't talk to anyone about it, so his pain was internalized.

16

GINA

*R*unning out of the hospital felt like the right thing to do. Gina couldn't believe that after she fought with herself to forgive Burnah for what he's done to her, he goes and pulls this shit. Burnah couldn't be faithful and she was tired of trying to be with a man who only thought of himself and spread his dick around like peanut butter. She wiped the tears from her face with her hands and headed to her mother's house in Baldwin Hills. Since she decided to transfer to *UCLA*, she was going to be staying there again. Gina hadn't told her older sister and brother that she was moving back. It was because she was homesick and she was stupid enough to want to be close to Burnah. This pain she was feeling in this moment had her wanting to hightail it back to *Grambling*. She couldn't believe that she walked in on that nurse sucking him off. Burnah was so nasty and disrespectful that she couldn't ever see herself being with him again.

€€€€€€€

Three days passed and Gina was in her bed, still mad with herself for loving this man. All she did was shower, eat and lie in the bed all day. There was nothing else that she wanted to do. Her mother tried to pry and ask her what was wrong, but she didn't tell her. All Gina wanted to do was mope for a little while. She felt like she was justified in feeling hurt. Her heart was broken and she needed some time to herself. Burnah had been blowing up her phone, but she never answered any of his calls or texts. He wasn't the romantic type, so she didn't expect any flowers or gifts to be sent. She was actually relieved for that because all of it would've been returned to him. The type of man that all of her family had warned her about was the type that she fell head over heels for. Burnah was like her lover and friend all wrapped into one. Now, she had to cut ties for her own self-worth.

As she sat in her bed looking at the ceiling, her eyes got hit with a burst of sunlight. She had to squint because it was so bright. Gina had black-out curtains to keep sunlight out. That meant that someone was in her room and had opened her curtains and blinds. She was too dejected to even see who it was.

"Munchie, what the hell is wrong with you? Mommy called and said you been in here moping and why aren't you going back to Texas?" Gina recognized the voice as her older sister, Gretchen.

"Nothing. I just want to be alone." she replied and tried to cover her face with a pillow to drown the sunlight out. Gretchen wasn't having that. She snatched the pillow up and threw it on the floor.

"Come on, GG! Leave me alone. I just want to lay here and chill. Why is that so bad?" Small streaks of tears started coming from her eyes.

"Ohmigosh, Munch, what is wrong, baby girl?" Gretchen kicked off her Nike Mother of Pearl KD 8s and jumped in the bed with her little sister.

"I let the wrong man have my heart." Gina confessed, in between her tears.

"Awwww, my poor baby. I know that it hurts. I thought you weren't dating anyone in Texas?" Gretchen asked, with deep confusion in her face and voice.

"I'm not with anyone in Texas." Gina responded, a little above a whisper.

"Well, who is it?" GG was puzzled and needed some clarification.

"Burnah...I've been messing with him for a little over a year." Gina revealed, causing Gretchen to let out an involuntary gasp from her throat.

"Are you serious right now, Munch? Why didn't you tell me?"

"I didn't want Gallardo and Zip to know. You know how overprotective they are of me."

"I never would've told ya secret." Gretchen was a little hurt that Gina didn't come to her.

"I know. I just got caught up and now, I just wish I never met him so that I wouldn't feel this way. I feel just like that Heather Headley song, I Wish I Wasn't."

"What happened?"

"I walked in on one of the nurses sucking his dick. Like how lowdown can you be?" Gina raised her voice a little, in anger.

"Ugh, that is nasty. I knew Burnah wasn't shit. I can't stand his young ass." GG rolled her eyes.

"Join the club. I can't believe I gave him my heart. I'm so pissed with myself. Like what do them bitches have that I don't? I was good to this nigga."

"These bitches are ready to take ya spot at a moment's notice. I'm mad you didn't tell me that you were fucking him, but I see why. Boss up on that nigga lil sis! Peep game because these niggas have community dick. Don't let him see you sweat." Gretchen schooled Gina on men and
the way they were.

"You're right, sis. I'm tired of crying over this nigga." Gina swatted her eyes with tissue.

"I know, baby girl. Clean ya face up and we about to go to the mall. Gallardo decided to treat the family to a shopping spree." Gretchen pointed out, hoping that would put a smile on her little sister's face.

"Yassss!" Gina got out of the bed and went to the bathroom to wash her face and shower.

She was happy about this shopping spree. Retail therapy was always a cure for the blues. No, it wouldn't mend her broken heart, but it would be nice to be around her family. She also still had Burnah's black card and was about to run his pockets for all of the stress he put her through.

€€€€€€€

Gina's best friend, Kienna finally moved to California and she decided to cheer Gina up. She was still down in the dumps, but slowly bouncing back from the heartbreak that she dealt with. Kienna knew how it felt to deal with an ain't shit nigga and knew her best needed a pick me up. They were enjoying food and drinks at *Lariders*. The place was packed from wall-to-wall. They were having a good time and Kienna was happy for that.

"Yassss bitchhhh!" Kienna yelled out, as Gina twerked to some song called *Fuck It Up* by a new artist named Rich Broke.

The DJ was playing the song and it was a hit with the ladies and dudes in there.

Fuck It Up, Fuck It Up,
Fuck It Up, Fuck It Up,
Streets Need Pure Dope No Rerock...

The song blared through the speakers and Gina didn't miss a single drop in the beat. Kienna joined her and they had the attention of most of the men and women in the building. Kienna was a professional dancer, fitness instructor, and choreographer. She knew that her body and moves were on point. They put on a show and danced until they were ready to head home.

Gina pulled out her phone and requested an Uber. Both herself and Kienna were drunk off their asses and didn't want to chance getting a DUI charge. The *LAPD* was always racist and ruthless and they were not with the shits. They just decided it would be better to just pick up their car in the morning. Kienna and Gina stood outside of the club, waiting for their ride. Dudes were trying to holla, but they weren't paying them any mind.

The Uber driver showed up and stopped at the curb. The Uber smelled like pure Cali Kush and Creed Aventus cologne. It was a matte black Mercedes-Benz G Wagon. The ladies jumped in and shut the door. What stood out the most about getting in the car, was that the driver was playing soft music.

"Ay, wassup," the driver turned to them and greeted.

His eyes were bloodshot red and low. Gina looked at him and recognition set in.

"Humble? Since when did you become an Uber driver? " Her voice slurred, but this came as a surprise.

"Shit, it's something I do to kill time. Good evening." He smiled, directing his greeting to Kienna.

"Hey, how you doing?" Kienna spoke back to Humble, liking what she saw.

"Unt uhn, Humble. Don't be...don't be trying to fuck with my best friend. You run with them Militia niggas and y'all don't know how to keep y'all dicks in ya pants."

"I'm not like that. I mean, I do have sex with females, but I'm a single man." Humble defended himself from Gina's allegations.

"That's what they all say." Gina was not letting up, considering that she was mad as hell at Burnah.

Call her bitter, but she didn't care one bit. She wouldn't let any of the crew mess over Kienna.

"Ay, gone on somewhere with all that shit, Munchie. Now, where I'm taking y'all? I gotta get back on the block." Humble was growing frustrated of her and the things she was saying.

"Is my brother out there?" Gina inquired, ignoring the fact that Humble was getting mad.

"Sis, chill out." Kienna warned her.

"I'm good."

"Yeah, he out there."

"Well, we are riding with you. I'll get him to drive us home." Gina insisted, with a wry smile on her face.

"Cool." Humble murmured and the rest of the car ride was quiet.

Gina's head was lowkey spinning from all of the liquor she

consumed, but the plan she had in her head, outweighed her state of drunkenness. Nothing was going to stop her from getting her vindication and revenge against Burnah. She wanted him to feel all of the hurt she was feeling. Her heart felt like it broke into pieces like shards of glass. She was feeling a range of emotions, but the rage was more apparent than all of them.

€€€€€€€

They made it to the block and Humble parallel parked his black G-Wagon on the side. He left the truck without any words.

"Ay, sis, I know that you're mad about what happened between you and Burnah, but you can't take it out on everybody else." Kienna chastised Gina.

"I know...I'm just so hurt...I guess it's like that saying...hurt people, hurt people."

"Well, you're going to have to work through that hurt."

"You're right." Gina wiped the tears that were starting to pool in her eyes and got out of the car.

She saw a loose brick sitting on the ground and picked it up. Everything happened so fast that she walked over to Burnah's Aston Martin and threw the brick through his windshield. The sound of his alarm blaring on the quiet residential street, piqued everyone's attention. They all saw the brick stuck in the middle of the windshield. All of their eyes from Burnah to Gina and back again.

He was so heated that he thought about fucking Gina up, but he remembered that her brother was out there and he didn't hit females. Burnah hobbled over to her with his cane and she met him in the middle of the street.

"What the fuck is ya problem, Gina? You need to take ya ass home with this bullshit on ya mind! Get ya drunk ass on! I can't believe you threw a brick through my fucking car!" Burnah spat, spittle coming from his mouth, in his anger.

"Fuck this raggedy ass piece of shit! You...you..played with my heart, so payback is a bitch!"

"Ya ass is fucking crazy!"

"You're right! I WAS CRAZY ENOUGH TO DEAL WITH YA COMMUNITY DICK HAVING ASS! YOU AIN'T SHIT!" Gina hollered out, making sure everyone could hear her.

She saw Gallardo standing there with a deep scowl and disappointment, but still decided to keep reading Burnah, so he could see just how she felt.

"YOU KNEW WHAT IT WAS! YEAH IT WAS FUCKED UP HOW YOU WALKED IN ON THAT, BUT WE NOT TOGETHER!" Burnah decided to do some yelling of his own, so they were in a shouting match right in the road.

"I was naive as fuck to give you my heart and pussy way back when. My heart is cold now and you have to deal with the fact that you had a real one and lost her to a scraggly hoe that can't even be there for you when the chips fall. You broke me and I let you." Tired of embarrassing herself, Gina walked off and headed back to Humble's G-Wagon.

Kienna was standing outside and pulled Gina into her arms as soon as she made it close to her. She cried tears of sorrow as every man there was frozen, in shock. They were anticipating what was about to happen. They knew how Gallardo felt about his sister, so it was only a matter of time before he snapped out of his trance.

"Humble, take them the fuck to my crib and wait there!" Gallardo was steaming mad and making his way over to Burnah.

"Aight, boss man." Humble jogged over to the truck and drove off.

Gina laid her head in Kienna's lap and went to sleep. She had enough excitement for the night. She knew that Gallardo was going to flip whenever he made it to his house. All she was hoped was that he had mercy on Burnah. No matter what, he was still a big part of her life and you can't just turn off feelings like that. She didn't know how long she would be hurting, but she knew that she didn't want anything remotely bad happening to him, either. All she could do is continue to live her life and hope that the pain alleviated

Gallardo

"So, you failed to tell me that you were fucking with my baby sister! Lil nigga, you got me fucked up!" Gallardo balled up his fists and sent one crashing into Burnah's jaw.

Burnah stumbled back a little from the impact of the punch. He had blood trickling from his lips and mouth. He couldn't even be mad because he knew how overprotective G was when it came to his sisters.

"Aight, I deserve that." Burnah spit blood onto the asphalt and stood there, staring at Gallardo.

"Nigga, you deserve way more than that. How long you been fucking with my sister?" It was taking everything in him not to full out his heat and give him an early funeral.

"Like a year...shit just happened." Burnah revealed, holding his jaw because it stung from the blow to his face, a few seconds before.

"Shit just happened? What the fuck are you, a *Lifetime* side bitch movie. How the fuck you just smash my sister and didn't give a nigga a clue?"

"She was asking me not to tell you." Burnah defended himself, feeing himself getting mad.

"I don't give a fuck what she told you. Yo' ass should have given me some kind of knowledge to this shit. You my nigga, so I'm only going to tell you this once, stay the fuck from my sister. Judging by how her drunk ass just pulled a Brandi from *A Thin Line Between Love And Hate* and *A Dairy of A Mad Black Woman* mixed together...let's me know you fucked up!"

"Man, that shit is over." Burnah murmured, spitting blood and saliva from his mouth.

"Better be. I'm not playing with you, Burnah. I'm about to get the fuck out of here, my high is blown." Gallardo scoffed and headed to his blacked out Benz CLS-20.

He didn't know what his destination was going to be, but he knew he couldn't go home. Gina was there and he couldn't even look at her.

Gallardo never wanted her to get mixed up with any nigga was claiming the streets as his occupation. He knew the hurt that his sister was registered on her face because he was responsible for that same hurt on many females over the years. He wanted something better for his little Munchie bear. She was the good girl, the youngest of the camp. This Burnah situation had him pissed.

Hopping on the 710, Gallardo smoked a joint of moon rocks and sipped on some Hennessy that he purchased from a liquor store in Inglewood. This was the only thing that would mellow him out. He had a condo he was subletting out there and nobody was currently staying in it. It was a smart investment move of many he had made over the years. He didn't have to stay in this life, but the Black Heart Militia was all that he knew. He didn't know if he could just give up everything that himself and his father built.

Too many men ate from the profits of their empire and put their blood, sweat, and life on the line just to chase the almighty dollar. He also knew that he would get heavy opposition from his dad. "OD," which is what the streets call him, would not be happy. All of this mess with his sister, them not figuring out who it was that shot at them at *IHOP*, and the fact that Gallardo felt like a big target was on his back, had him seriously thinking of just leaving it all behind. Nobody ever knew what kind of stress went into being the "King Of Compton". The shit wasn't a cakewalk. It was stressful to get to reaping those rewards.

Arriving at his condo, Gallardo parked into the garage and entered the house through the door. He disarmed the alarm and headed down the hallway past two of the bedrooms and the laundry room. The lights automatically turned on whenever you entered a room and flicked off whenever you exited that room. He made it to the kitchen and dumped the contents of his pocket. All he had was his cellphone, the bag of moon rock weed, a pack of Winterfresh gum, and some business card he received from a Navy recruiter as he was leaving the light bill place from paying a few people in the hood's bills. He did it every month. The recruiter was standing out there and was passing them to every young man he saw. Gallardo pocketed the card, but the Navy was furthest from his mind. He didn't understand why he wasn't throwing the card away. Instead, he just kept it lying there on the granite countertop.

Gallardo grabbed a water bottle from the fridge and made a mental reminder to pick up some groceries to go in the condo. He would be here for a few days because he needed the time to cool off. He also would use this time to hang with Nik Nik and her son, Naheem. They talked and texted all the time, since the day that he took her lunch to the hospital. It was crazy because things like that were out of character for him. Him buying you *McDonald's* would be special. Gallardo was not into the whole wining and dining of females. Especially, if all she was doing is swallowing or riding the ten inches in his jeans. Other than that, he felt like they had nothing to talk about. Women equated getting fed to a man wanting to be with them and Gallardo was not falling in that trap. He let every woman know that he was just fucking and nothing more. That's why he couldn't understand why Mia was trippin'. It wasn't like she didn't know the game. This was the same bitch who was pushing an Aston Martin and didn't have a fucking job, at all. He was confused by her reaction. To solve all of that, he blocked her from calling and texting him.

€€€€€€€

"Right on time, I see." Nikayla gave him her beautiful smile.

"When I tell you I will be somewhere, then I'm there." Gallardo responded, grabbing her up into a hug.

It was the afternoon and Gallardo promised Nikayla that he would be taking her and Naheem out somewhere, the day before. She was surprised that he was so punctual. Most men she dated, showed up late and then acted nonchalant about it. He said he would be there at five o' clock and he show up at five o' clock on the dot.

"I'm glad to see that. You can come in. I have to finish getting ready," Nik Nik informed him, as she opened the door wider for him to gain entry. "You can chill out here. GG should be in soon, with Naheem. She went to pick him up from extended day."

"Aight, cool." Gallardo sat on the couch and grabbed the remote to the TV.

He settled the TV on the Investigation Discovery Channel and killed time.

He was focused on some show with lions, until he heard the front door open. He laid eyes on his little sister and cute kid, who he knew to be Naheem, walking into the apartment. The little boy whizzed past him and ran to the back of the house.

"Naheem, you better slow your little behind down in here." GG chastised her godson.

"Yes ma'am!" Naheem obliged his mother and slowed down.

"Wassup, bighead." Gretchen mushed her big brother in the head.

"Shit. Just picking up Nik Nik and Naheem. You?"

"Nothing much...just tired as hell. About to take a nice bubble bath, sip some wine, and go to bed." She yawned as she took a seat next to her brother.

"You knew about Burnah and Munchie?"

"She just told me yesterday. I was so shocked. He fucked things up. I heard you beat his ass on the block."

"I had no choice. He violated for real." Gallardo let out a deep sigh.

"Well, you did what you had to do. I just can't believe that our little sister kept this secret for so long. We don't hold secrets from each other. It's been like that since we all were kids."

"Yeah...guess she's growing up and me and Zip gotta cut the reins loose. I just never thought she would end up with that lil nigga. He must be had a hold on her."

"Must be. So, you really like my best?" GG questioned her brother, seriously.

"Yeah, I do. On some real shit, I can see a future with her. She's dope as hell."

"Just don't hurt her. She's been through a lot— her and Naheem." GG warned Gallardo.

"I got them." Gallardo responded, seriously.

They stopped talking when they heard footsteps coming toward the front of the apartment. It was Nikayla and Naheem.

"We're ready now," she announced, with a smile.

Gallardo stood up, so he could look at Nikayla for a second. She was so beautiful and her eyes were hypnotic. His were hazel with honey undertones, while hers were hazel, but had some green undertones in them.

"You look really beautiful." Gallardo pulled her into a hug.

"You don't look too bad yourself." Nik Nik gave him a peck on the lips.

"Ewwww, y'all gonna get cooties!" Naheem teased and pretended to gag.

"Boy, bye." Nikayla playfully hit him on the head.

They said their goodbyes to GG and headed out of the door, to Gallardo's Porsche Cayenne SUV. Gallardo helped Nikayla into the truck, taking advantage of getting free reign to touch her butt.

"Better stop starting stuff you can't finish," Nikayla whispered to him.

"Who said that I can't." Gallardo winked at her and went to the drivers side to get in.

Nikayla leaned over and opened the door for him. That had Gallardo impressed. His mother told him about the "door test" but he never had a female ever do it for him before this day.

He hopped in the truck and made his way to the Santa Monica Pier. That's where he was taking them since it was a school night and already pushing close to six o' clock.

€€€€€€€

"So, what do you see yourself doing in the future?" Nikayla queried,
as they walked

along the beach together.

The sun was going down and they were watching Naheem as he ran around flying the remote control drone that Gallardo bought him from one of the shops on the pier. They rode the rides, ate junk food and dinner, and just enjoyed themselves. Gallardo was happy to see the smiles on both of their faces. He even more content with seeing the smile reaching Nikayla's eyes this time. He knew she had a story and hoped she shared it with him one of these days.

"Shit, I haven't really thought that far. Honestly, I just like to see my people straight. I rarely think of me, on some real G shit." Gallardo confided to Nikayla.

"Why is that? You don't think you need an exit strategy if shit gets too crazy in this game."

"Not really."

"You know you're acting just like...," Nikayla's voice trailed off and she stopped walking.

Gallardo came behind her and wrapped his arms around her body. He leaned down, so that his chin could rest on the top of her head.

"What was you about to say?"

"It's really nothing." Nik Nik tried to end the conversation, but Gallardo was very persistent when he felt like someone was holding back from him.

"It's definitely something because yo' whole vibe changed. Talk to me, Nik Nik."

"My ex, Nathan...he had the same way of thinking. He's dead now."

"That's Naheem's dad, right? What happened to him?"

"He robbed some banks and the police killed him. He was trying to impress his brother, who was a Crip. He's been gone for about three years now." Nikayla remarked, sadly.

She still held some sadness for the way things ended for Nathan and the fact that he would never see his son, deep in her heart. Hearing Gallardo speak so bleakly about his life, made her think back to the rough times she had after Nathan's death.

"Damn, I'm sorry to hear that. I was just being honest with

ya...I've never had any plans. I just knew at some point I would need to get out...just not sure how I was going to go about it."

"You have to find something that you are passionate about, love." Nikayla surmised, letting out a sigh and wiping the tears from her eyes.

"This Navy recruiter gave me this card a while ago and I've been holding on to it. The military never been something I thought about, but for some reason I can't get rid of the card." He revealed, staring out at the water and the waves slamming against the rocks.

"Maybe God is trying to tell you something."

"I don't know. Let's get out of here...it's getting pretty dark and I'm sure little man needs to get ready for bed."

"Okay."

They walked down the pier and headed back to Gallardo's truck. He turned his radio to a soft jazz station and they rode to Nikayla's house in silence. Gallardo was thinking about the things that Nikayla said to him. No one had ever had him see things a different way, besides his mother and sister, Gretchen. Maybe keeping that card was a sign that he needed to get out of the game. He didn't know for certain, but he had a feeling if he stuck with Nikayla, she would have him thinking of more possibilities for his life. Until then, he was going to keep running the empire that he had on his shoulders. He couldn't leave Zip and his niggas behind.

17

NEHEMIAH

*N*ehemiah sat in the driver's seat of his old 2008 Chevy Impala, nursing a bottle of *Old English* malt liquor. It was his second bottle of the day. He was spying on Nikayla, Gallardo, and Naheem. He was jealous that she was giving him the time of day. He had wanted Nikayla since the day that his brother, Nathan brought her to their mother's house to meet her. He hated Nikayla now because she turned her nose to him. It was the main reason why he made his brother rob the banks, with the notion that he would become a Crip. Nehemiah never was going to let his little brother join the gang. He knew that he would never get away with the task he gave him.

He turned the bottle up and focused on them as they played at the park. He knew who Gallardo was because he had killed his homies. He had a plan to get at Gallardo and rape Nikayla. The woman who sat next to him, in the passenger side sniffing cocaine was going to help him with his plans. She was a woman scorned and a woman scorned didn't give a fuck who she hurt in her wake. Nehemiah stared at Mia with lust in his eyes. They had been fucking for about a few weeks now and he had to say that she was the best piece of ass that he ever had. Between sniffing the blow, popping mollies, and drinking, Mia was another high that he was happy to indulge in.

"I still hate that bitch for thinking that she could be with anyone, but me." Nehemiah thought he was talking to himself, but ended up saying it out loud.

"Well, we are even...the bitch stole my man. My sister says that she acts like she the shit. I'm ready to knock her ass off of her pedestal." Mia spat, envy dripping from her statement.

"Well, we gotta our this plan in motion and make sure it's foolproof. This nigga offed a few of the homies and I'm not letting that shit ride. That's on the set!" Nehemiah took another sip from the 40oz bottle.

"I say we do a series of shit and then keep escalating."

"Damn, I like the way you think. Me and my niggas about to make these soft ass *Black Mask Militia* niggas feel us for the old and new."

"That's the shit I like to hear." Mia laughed and sniffled a little from the drugs making her nose runny.

Tired of looking at the two of them, Nehemiah drove off, happy that he was finally going to be close to taking out the Black Heart Militia and their leader. He also was anticipating feeling if Nikayla's pussy was as good as Nathan used to describe it, when he was alive.

The *Black Mask Militia* was living on borrowed time and didn't even know it. He had Mia working on Burnah, making her think that her name was Tasha. Gallardo didn't know that she was a nurse and none of the other men had ever seen her. This was working in his favor and would contribute to the fall of their crew. Pussy could make niggas act out of character and that was what he was hoping for.

18

ZIP

*Z*ip sat in his living room, lying down as Zasaya sat on the other side of the sectional, watching *Monsters Inc.* Zip was dealing with a cold and her mother, Saya was MIA. She had been at his Long Beach home for three weeks now. When he went to Saya's apartment to see what was wrong with her, the apartment looked like it had been unattended for weeks. The place smelled sour from the food that was going bad, due to the lights being shut off. This wasn't like Saya to just leave without a notice. She may have not been the best girlfriend or babymama, but she took care of her daughter. It was no doubt to Zip that she loved her.

He was battling a fever of 101 degrees and barely could keep anything down. Despite everything going on, he refused to go to the hospital and to call anyone for help. He felt like drinking his *DayQuil* and *NyQuil*, eating canned chicken noodle soup, and rubbing his chest with Vicks Vapor Rub would help him feel better.

"Daddy, you want me to call auntie Serita?" Zasaya inquired, referring to his cousin, Gallardo's mother.

"Nawww...cough...achoo...I'm good baby girl." Zip whined, feeling so miserable.

"Auntie Serita will make you feel all better, Daddy."

"I know, baby girl...cough...call this number for me?" Zip pointed to Suri's phone number in his phone.

Zasaya pressed the button on the phone. She placed it on speakerphone.

"Hello?" Suri came onto the line.

"Suri Uri...cough...cough...what are you doing?" Zip asked her, before falling into another coughing fit.

"I'm at work, finishing up a project. Zacarion, you don't sound too good." She voiced, with concern.

"Shit, I don't feel good at all." He managed to get out, in between coughs and sneezes.

"Oooohh, Daddy! You said a curse word!" Zasaya sang out.

"I'm sorry, baby girl." Zip apologized and took Suri off of speakerphone.

"Zacarion, I get off in about two hours. I will be there to help you. If you're still dramatic as you used to be back in the days..I know you acting like you're about to die." Suri laughed, causing Zip to suck his teeth.

"You ain't funny. It do feel like I'm about to die. I'm about to try to go to sleep until you come through. A nigga is tired for real." Zip let out a yawn at the same time.

"Okay. See you later." Suri hung up the phone and Zip lied back on the sofa.

Zasaya went back to her side of the sofa and resumed watching Monsters, Inc.

He honestly didn't want to get her sick, but Saya hadn't surfaced yet. He decided that he would call Gina to pick her up once he woke up. She was still in town and Zasaya loved hanging with her.

€€€€€€€

A few hours later...

Zip woke up, his shirt was soaking wet from him sweating in his sleep. He looked up and Suri was in the living room, watching some show on *Netflix*. He was confused as to how she got into the house. He also noticed at Zasaya wasn't sitting in the living room. He sat up and removed the shirt, showing off his washboard abs and the tattoos that adorned his chest. There were so many, but they were all intricate and had a meaning to him. Suri turned away from her show and was staring at Zip.

"Yo...Suri Uri, you good?" He looked at her because she was just sitting there, frozen.

Snapping out of her temporary lapse of lusting over him, Suri replied, "Yeah, I'm good. You're burning up, if you're sweating like that and the air conditioner is on."

"Yeah, I feel so damn hot. Like I'm in hell or some shit. How did you get in here?" He was still confused about that part.

"Your cousin, Gina let me in when she came to pick up Zasaya. She is too pretty." Suri complimented his daughter and answered his question.

"Oh, shit. A nigga must have really been out for real."

"You're sick, so you're going to sleep a lot. I'm going to take care of you and nurse you back to health. First things first, I need you to go change into some dry clothes and I'll come up there, so you can lie in the bed."

"Aight." Zip got up from the sectional and headed upstairs.

He was standing in the middle of the bathroom, naked. He felt so hot that he didn't even want to put on clothes. He stood in the shower, under completely cold water. The inside of Zip's bathroom was soundproof and so was his shower, that was encased in its own glass box. His shower was big enough for five to ten people to be in there at once.

As he lathered his body with his Creed body wash. Suri walked into the bathroom. When she did, she got an eyeful of Zip's naked body. Even when he was on soft, his dick was still swinging. She didn't have to worry about him trying anything because he was sick and had no energy.

They made eye contact and Suri nearly stumbled on her own two feet, trying to leave out of the bathroom. She was a little flustered and definitely loved what she saw. She knew she had to play it cool and help him recover. This wasn't the time for her to jump his bones. There would definitely be a time for that, she thought, with a devious smile and a nibble of her bottom lip.

Despite not wanting to wear clothes, Zip emerged, dressed in some Ethika underwear and a Chicago Bulls t-shirt. That happened to be his favorite team. He put on some socks and went and got in his bed. The coughing and sneezing started back and Suri sprang into action, to help him be comfortable.

She grabbed all of the supplies she brought with her and started playing the doting nurse. The first thing she did was check his temperature.

"Your temp came up to 101.8...you're pretty hot."

"I feel like that shit too. My head hurting like a motherfucker." Zip whined, just like all sick men do.

"Here, take this." Suri passes him two *Theraflu* tablets and a bottle of Gatorade.

"Thank you." Zip accepted the medicine and the drink from her.

"No problem. I'll be back. Imma go fix you some soup." Suri kissed him on the head and left the room.

€€€€€€€

A week later...

"I gotta figure out some romantic shit to do for Suri tonight." Zip confided in his niggas, as they sat in their safe house in Downey.

They had just finished the list of foreign cars they had to steal. Everything went smoothly and now they were just laying low.

"Nothing says romantic like fucking in the rain, while Mystikal is playing. Angry dick is some romantic shit, bruh." Allure responded, confidently like he gave Zip the right solution.

"Nigga, what?" Zip looked at Allure like he was crazy.

"The shit work for me." Allure shrugged his shoulder and made his move on the pool table.

"Take her on a picnic." Humble replied, remembering the picnic he took Kienna on and how things got real nasty.

"If you wanna be real romantic, take her ass to one of these baseball fields and tell her that you enjoy getting yo' dick nicely tonsiled...see, romance. That's the nicest way to tell her to get lockjaw." Serry took a hit of the joint of Cali Kush he was blazing.

"I got a few hours to figure this shit out and you niggas are no help."

"Give her a massage with *IcyHot*. That shit works like a charm."

"You tried that shit before?" Zip asked, skeptically.

"Hell yeah. That shit is an aphrodisiac to these bitches." KB suggested, adding his two cents.

"I'm about to get the fuck outta here. Still gotta handle this other shit before I scoop Suri up. Y'all niggas is some fucking clowns." Zip walked out of the house and headed to his Maserati.

"You really tried that shit for real?" Serry asked KB.

"Naw. That nigga about to go do some dumb shit." KB shrugged and broke the balls on the pool table.

€€€€€€€

Zip and Suri ended up at his house for a special dinner. When she walked in, there were orange and red roses spread all over the place. Mr. Ferimo looked out for him for the flowers. He was their go to man when it came to all things related to horticulture. When Zip laid eyes on the flowers in *In Full Bloom,* he knew they were the perfect ones for him. He wanted to do things right when it came to Suri this time. Honestly, he regretted how he let Saya and other things fog him from what was real. Suri was down for him and he messed that all up for a hoe. It was the typical hood love story. Almost all dopeboys have fell for a hoe. It was who they seemed to attract when they were being flashy and on the scene.

Seeing the expression on Suri's face from the set up he had in his living room, made it worthwhile. In addition to the flowers, he had a table set for two. He even brought out the pots and pans for this occasion. His aunt, Serita taught himself, Gallardo, Gina, and Gretchen how to cook. All of them could cook some shit up that would make you think you in a restaurant or something.

"Zacarion, this is so beautiful! Thank you." Suri gave him a peck on the lips and they went to sit down at the table.

Zip pulled her chair out and was acting like a complete gentleman.

"I'll be back. Gotta go get this food."

He went into the kitchen and plated the Cajun lemon butter salmon, homemade seafood macaroni and cheese, and garlic veggie stir fry he made. The food smelled good and he knew that Suri would appreciate it. He used to cook for her when they were friends. Hell, she was the only girl he ever cooked for.

He placed a plate in front of her and sat his down.

"This smells so good. Damn, I forgot how much I missed your cooking!" Suri let out a moan that had Zip's dick rocking up.

"Shit I haven't cooked in a while. A nigga always on the go and eating fast food and shit.

What you want to drink?"

"You got some Moscato?"

"Yeah, I picked you up some of that girly ass shit. A whole damn bottle." Zip teased, going in the kitchen to grab her bottle, a wine glass, and his bottle of Ciroc.

He poured the drinks and they said grace. After that, they both dumb into the food. They fell in a comfortable silence as they ate. Both of them had things on their mind and weren't ready to address them. The silence seemed like the best thing.

"Ay, I know that ya haven't been back here that long, but I wanna see how fucking with ya on an exclusive level would work." Zip blurted out, as he took the last few bites of his food.

"Wow! I wasn't expecting that. Are you sure that's what you want?" Suri questioned, seriously.

Zip had her undivided attention in that moment. She wanted to make sure he was sure. His track record for being faithful wasn't that good. She wasn't the type to share or deal with a nigga that thought he was going to.

"Hell yeah. Never been more sure about anything in my life." Zip replied, looking her dead in the eyes.

She could see the sincerity in them, but wasn't sure if she should take it there with him. She knew how baby mamas could be, damn that, she knew how Saya could be. She was a very childish woman. Suri didn't have time for the drama, so she was confirming that Zip knew what was up.

"I only want ya ass for real. You can be my bad ass Woman Crush Everyday out this bitch." They both shared a laugh at him being silly.

"You better make certain you sure. I'll be quick to pull that photo of "only your limbs shit" on Facebook because I refuse to be with someone with community dick...now, if you make me look stupid, imma make you look dead."

"Damn, ya ass done went to New York and turned into a savage. Let me find out my bitch on that gangsta shit." Zip chuckled and stood up from his seat.

"You ain't know? A bitch was born and raised in Compton. I don't play that dumb shit." Suri replied, sassily.

"Check you out." Zip grabbed her face and they engaged in a kiss with a little tongue.

Suri broke the kiss and they just stared at each other. They were finished with dinner, so Zip put the dishes up and ushered her to his room. In there, he had roses all over the place and music playing. Eric Bellinger's *Drive By* was playing softly from the Pandora station on his Smart TV.

"I wanna give you a massage. Drop that dress." Zip commanded, going into the restroom to prepare for the massage.

He pulled out the tube of *Icy Hot* from the *Walmart* bag and opened the package. He placed a decent amount on his hands to rub Suri down with. He was trying to be romantic, but it soon backfired.

"Damn, this shit is hot as fuck! This the last time I listen to that dumb ass nigga, KB!" Zip griped as his hands felt like they were on fire.

"Zacarion, what's wrong with you?" Suri looked at him with her face etched in deep concern.

"Fuckkkk, NOTHING!" He didn't mean to yell, but the hotness of his hands was making him mad.

Just as he was about to go rinse the cream off of his hands, it went cold. Zip was mad as hell. Suri walked into the bathroom to see what was going on.

"Zacarion, what happened? Why are ya in here yelling?"

For a second, he was entranced by the thick and petite body before him. He snapped out

of his reverie because his hands were starting to feel uncomfortably cold.

"I was trying to give you a massage because my nigga said that *Icy Hot* was some good shit to rub someone down with."

"What the hell? Which one of them fools told you that? Don't even tell me...KB?" Suri remarked, finding humor in this situation.

"Yeah, it was that nigga."

"I think he set you up." Suri laughed and put him on *Snapchat*.

"Imma beat that nigga ass." Zip snapped, playfully.

"Y'all niggas still some fools. Imma definitely love being home."

"I'm glad for that shit because I'm not letting ya ass leave." Zip was dead ass serious with his last statement.

He was in this thing for the long haul and Suri would soon find out just how serious he was.

It was eight o' clock at night and the sun was going down and he was camped out, waiting for her to leave. KB stood at Thai's back door and broke in. It didn't take much for him to do it. The door was flimsy and easy to get into if you knew how to pick locks. KB was hood bred, so all hood niggas had some knowledge in getting into doors that they needed to get in, even if their survival was at risk. She lived in an apartment on Slauson Ave. so he didn't have to worry about meddling neighbors calling one time out there. They weren't trying to have *LAPD* all in their shit out there. He was sure of that. KB made sure that she left for her shift at the hospital. She worked from nine p.m. to nine a.m. nowadays, so it wa easy for him to sneak in when she wasn't home at night.

Once he made it in, he could smell the Twilight Woods wall things she plugged in around the house. The place was also spotless. He didn't expect anything less of her. Thai always kept things neat like she was OCD or something. He missed her and hadn't talked to her much since they had that sex session in the bathroom at the hospital. The one night she did let him take her out, she stopped the date because he slapped the hell out of some old man who he accused of staring at her ass. Come to find out, the old man was blind, but KB didn't feel like he should apologize. It was a simple mistake on his part. He walked through the house and saw that she had two messages on her answering machine. Thailand was the only young girl that KB knew that still had a landline. He just found it funny. He went to the machine and checked the messages. He listened to both messages as if they were left for him and this was his house.

Hey Thai, this is Mona! I don't care about why you came to LA. All I know is that your little ass better be on that plane tomorrow for your niece's birthday party. None of us will have any understanding if you're not there. It will be at Henre's house in Jersey. It's a new place, so I will email you the address. Hope to see you there! I miss my main bish! The plane ticket is at the Delta kiosk in LAX. I love you sissy. Bye.

The next message low key had KB pissed.

Hi, Ms. Reynolds. The pregnancy test results were correct after all. I need you to call the doctor's office at (310)863-4532 to talk about options and additional tests that need to be taken. Have a wonderful evening.

So that's why this bitch been avoiding me? KB mused to himself, feeling his anger rising. He had to leave her house. It was a must. He would hack her email as well so that he could get the flight information. Thailand had him fucked up if she thought that he was going to keep playing these games with him. He would be right at Delta whenever the flight was. The fuck she thought this was. He turned the answering machine back off and remarked the messages as unread. KB slipped out of the door just as quietly as he came in. He ended up with more than what he came for. He just knew that he was going to be killing a nigga for touching what was his. Thai still didn't understand that she was stuck with him. KB was going to make that perfectly clear the next day.

The next day, KB went to go pick up his ticket from the Delta Arlines service desk and then headed through TSA so he could head on his flight. KB walked through the airport whistling and carrying on as if he was supposed to be there. He noticed the lustful stares he was getting and he even knew some of the women peeped the bulge in his gray sweats. He wore them so he could be comfortable on the flight. He made to the gate and he was just in the nick of time. The plane was leaving within the next five minutes.

"Hey, sir. Glad you made it. We were just about to take off."

"My bad. TSA was taking a little longer than usual." KB gave the lady a smile.

"Okay, now let's hustle so you can make your flight."

KB carried his backpack and boarded the plane. He walked through his assigned seat and Thai wasn't paying attention. KB unzipped his bag and pulled out his Beats by Dre wireless headphones, his Gatorade, and a pack of Starburst. He placed the bag up in the overhead compartment. Thai turned when he was done with the bag. She was in for a rude awakening when she saw KB sitting down.

"How the hell did you know I was on this flight?"

"I got my ways," KB replied, opening his Starburst candy. "Want some?" He was offering her some of the candy.

"Hell naw, I don't want any candy! I wanna know why you are following me. I told you
whatever this was, was over."

"That's where you wrong...when you let me hit that, it became mine." KB was calm, despite the apparent attitude that she had.

"Ughhhhh! I can't stand you!" Thailand rolled her eyes and looked out of the window.

"Chill out before I fuck the shit out of you in that little ass bathroom." KB threatened and grabbed his dick for emphasis, causing Thailand to gasp.

"Oh my!" The flight attendant had walked by and heard what KB said to her.

She kept walking, but her face was red.

"You need to move out of my way because I'm getting the fuck off of this plane! I don't see how you thought it was cool for you to just come on this flight with me!" Thai got up from the seat and tried to get past KB.

"Why the fuck you being difficult? I'm on the plane so that's the end of this discussion!"

"I don't care how you feel. Your stalker ass need to leave me alone!" People were starting to look at them as they yelled back and forth.

They were causing a big scene and the plane hadn't even took off yet.

"Ma'am, you have to sit down, the plane is about to take off." The flight attendant advised Thai, who was still standing up and looking like she wanted to take his head off.

"Sit yo' ass down!" KB gave her this hardened look, but she scowled right back at him.

"Fuck you!" Thai shot up her middle finger.

"All you gotta do is slide to the bathroom with a nigga!" KB chuckled and blew her a kiss.

"You won't ever taste this again!" She snapped, rolling her eyes at him.

"You got me fucked up! Now, shut up. A nigga plan to sleep during this flight." KB placed his Beats on his ears and closed his eyes.

He honestly didn't care about Thailand's tantrum. She was pregnant with his seed and didn't realize how stuck she was. Not even she could tell him that it was over. Someone would have to kill him in order for that to be possible. That child in her belly, solidified that they were a couple. No, KB wasn't the settling down type, but for his child, he was willing to try. This child would not have the same childhood he had. Bouncing from foster home to foster home and not knowing where his next meal was, was not in the cards for this child.

They had a five hour flight and KB was going to take that time to sleep. He hadn't been getting much of that due to the *Black Heart Militia* business he was handling. Himself, Zip, Humble, and Serry took care of the drug distribution and foreign car theft parts of the Militia, while Tress went to school and dealt with the surveillance and security part of the crew. Gallardo handled everything, but diamond brokering was his specialty. He was good at it, so everyone let him deal with it. He also liked the suit and tie look, while the rest of them preferred a white tee, Levi's hanging slightly off their ass, and Chucks on their feet.

KB had been spending all his time in the streets, so this rest away from LA was something that he needed. He also wanted to get to know more about Thai. He couldn't put his finger on it, but she was slowly making her way to his heart. It didn't matter that he wasn't the committing type or that she acted like she didn't want him. She had no choice, in his eyes.

€€€€€€€

Once the flight landed, they exited the plane and headed to baggage claim to grab their luggage. KB didn't allow Thailand to carry anything, but their carry-ons. After she tried to make another scene, he told her to shut the fuck up and they proceeded to walk over to the area where they were supposed to be waiting on the girl, Mona. Thai avoided any contact with him as they sat on the bench outside of the airport. KB let her have her little tantrum and took out his phone to check on what was happening back home. He didn't like being out the loop. He wanted to know everything that was going on in case he had to cut this trip short.

A few minutes later, an all-white Range Rover pulled up to the curb. The windows had limousine tint, so KB couldn't see who it was. The truck was really nice. As KB continued to silently admire the SUV, the door opened and a woman hopped out.

She was short and her skin was the color of some cocoa with a hint of cream. She had really curly hair and KB had to admit that she was sexy as hell.

Thai looked in the direction he was staring and rose up from the bench. She was smiling from ear-to-ear. She ran over to the woman and KB immediately assessed that she was Mona. He grabbed up the bags as the women hugged and caught up with one another.

"I'm glad you used that ticket because your brothers were getting on my damn nerves asking about you." KB heard Mona tell Thai.

"I wouldn't miss my niece's birthday for anything in the world."

"I know. You know they are going to kick your ass, right?" Mona looked at her, intently.

"Why?" Thai quizzed, with a confused look on her face.

"The fact that you have been gone for too long and him." Mona pointed at KB, who was standing there just observing their conversation.

"What about me?" KB asked, trying not to be rude.

"She's never mentioned that she was seeing anyone or anything. She has five brothers who are very overprotective of her." Mona warned him, with a smile.

"What's that supposed to mean to me. I hope you don't think I'm going to be scared." KB smiled, knowing that's what she was insinuating.

"I didn't mean it like that...I was just telling you about her brothers."

"Duly noted. My name is KB and you can call me KB." That rudeness was starting to rear its ugly head.

KB placed the bags in the trunk and sat in the backseat. He was quiet during the ride to the birthday party they were supposed to go to. Before making it to the house in New Jersey, they went to *Target*. Thai needed to pick up a gift for her niece and her other nieces and nephews. KB remained in the shadows and let Thai have a good time with her sister-in-law. He was sure he rubbed Mona the wrong way because she refused to have another conversation with him. He honestly didn't care, but if he was trying to be with Thai and raise their child, he needed to chill out and get to know her family.

They arrived at this big cobblestone home with a large circular driveway. KB was in awe at the place. They had nice houses in Los Angeles, but they looked nothing like the ones in New York and New Jersey. KB made a mental note to think about getting a place on the East Coast.

KB opened his door and opened Thai's door as well. She hopped out and thanked him. KB felt his stomach growl as he smelled the barbecue that cooking in the backyard. He could hear the music blaring from outside. This birthday party was lit. Mona opened the front door and the usual chaos that came with a birthday party was happening around them. There were kids running around playing and laughing. As they walked more and more into the house, he saw women in the kitchen, and the men were sitting in a den that had a pool table, a 70-inch screen TV and a large sectional.

"You can make yourself at home. Do you want something to drink?" Thai asked him, with an unreadable expression on her face.

"You can bring me a beer." KB responded, taking a seat on the far end of the sectional.

Thai disappeared from the den area and KB just sat there looking through his phone. Whatever conversation the men were having, it ceased when he walked into the room.

"Man, who the fuck are you?" One of the dudes in the room sized KB up, as they all sat in the den.

"Whoever the fuck Thai wants me to be." KB responded, refusing to back down to any of Thailand's family members.

"You think you funny, nigga?" The guy directed to KB, harshly.

"Yo' sister does," KB had no remnants of a smile or emotion on his face.

He feared no man and it wasn't going to start that day. The man approached him like they had beef, but someone held him back. KB had a smirk on his face.

"Ay, Buddah, chill your extra high strung ass down, so we can see who son is." The dude holding him back chastised the one about to come after KB.

"Naw, B, that nigga need to learn how to watch his fucking mouth. All I asked was a question." Buddah defended himself, with a scowl.

"I don't have to answer to you. Just because y'all niggas don't know me, don't mean imma be intimidated by any of you. Y'all bleed just like I do." KB stood up and looked Buddah directly at eye level.

"Ay, you need to chill, son. Our sister bring a random nigga around and you better believe we gonna ask about ya ass. Fuck outta here." Another one of her brothers were coming at KB wrong.

"I'm not yo' motherfucking son. That girl in there is carrying my seed. I don't know why y'all trying to hold this whack ass " intimidate the nigga because we her brothers" role. I ain't here for that. I'm here because she wanted to see y'all and whether I have y'all blessing or not, I'm here." KB said his peace and say back down.

Before he could say anything else, Buddah broke from the hold his brother had on him and jumped on KB. They began to engage in a fist fight that had everyone cringing. They were hitting each other so hard. Finally having enough, Buddah pulled his trusty .45 from his pocket and cocked it. He placed it up to KB's temple. The room was quiet and the bruhthers didn't know what to say or do to keep Buddah from pulling the trigger. He was the most overbearing one when it came to Thailand. Thailand and the rest of the ladies ran in the room when they heard all of the commotion.

"Ohmigosh, Buddah! What are you doing?" Thai yelled out, fear radiating from her voice.

"What am I doing? This nigga too disrespectful, yo!"

KB just sat there and stared at everyone in the room. He couldn't even be mad at Buddah. He probably would have reacted the same way if his little sister brought a nigga around and was pregnant by him.

"You can't do this?" Massika pleaded with Buddah.

"Big Booty, get the fuck on! This nigga violated." He pushed the gun into KB's temple, harder.

"Nigga, you better calm de fuck down and watch how you talk to me!" Massika slapped the shit out of him and Buddah removed the gun from his head.

"GET THE FUCK OUT! Thai you stay your ass here! " He yelled at KB and turned the coffee table over.

KB spit out the blood pooling in his mouth. He let out a hearty laugh and walked out of the house. He knew that if he didn't leave then he would be pulling out the gun he had behind his back. This wasn't how he planned to meet Thailand's family. He took an Uber away from the house, with no destination in sight. If Thailand thought that she was going to leave him, she had another thing coming. Her crazy family put no fear in his heart. He knew that her brothers would be in their feelings for a while, but he didn't give a flying fuck. He would give Thai a few days to marinate and then let her know what's up when they left back on their flight to LA. He leaned his head on the back of the seat and closed his eyes.

"That nigga got a hell of a right hook!" KB laughed, maniacally.

The Uber driver watched him from the rearview mirror.

"Yo, you good, bro?" He asked, his New York accent oozing with every word he spoke.

"Yeah, I'm good." KB glared at him and closed his eyes again.

The Uber driver focused back on the road and drove around New Jersey, until KB figured out a location.

As he was riding, his phone chimed. It was a message from Serry.

SERRY: THAT NIGGA, BURNAH GOTTA GO!

KB: WYM?

Serry: He broke Munchie's jaw on some dumb shit. Nigga was
higher than a kite.
KB: I'm on my way back to the hood.

"Ay, I need you drive this piece of shit, so I can get to the airport."

"Sure thing." The Uber driver sped up and headed toward the airport, with no hesitation.

20

MUNCHIE

*G*etting over Burnah was one of the hardest things that Gina had to do. After seeing him in that room and catching him getting head from the nurse, she realized that they did not need to be together. He was too toxic for her and probably could never change his dog ass ways. She wasn't even going to waste her time energy on the situation. Since she was back living in Cali, she was attending *UCLA* to finish her three years in business management. Her family, friends, and education were all that mattered to her these days. Why be with a nigga that was going to just think of himself, when you could stack your paper and wait for the man that God had for you?

That was Gina's mindset. In addition to her education, Gina's skin was glowing due to her vegetarian diet and working out with her best friend, Kienna. She had a nice body before, but now she was bodied. That was one of the perks of having a best friend who owned a workout/ pole fitness studio and her specialty was "making yo' last nigga regret not being with you."

Gina arrived at *Get Snatched!* and killed her engine. It was her birthday, but she was just content with working out and going home and drinking a glass of wine. She wasn't all that excited about her twenty-first birthday. GG, Nikayla, and Suri were meeting her for a birthday workout. That was the only request that Gina made to her family. Her mother did surprise her with her favorite cheesecake that morning and her father called her from jail and said she would be receiving something from him later in that day.

She had on her Nike workout gear and her Red October Yeezys. She opened the door and sauntered into the studio.

"SURPRISE!" Everyone yelled out, in excitement.

Gina was so happy that she dropped a few tears of joy, seeing all of her family and friends there, to help her celebrate her birthday. She was certainly surprised because they kept this tight-lipped from her.

"Ohmigosh! Y'all are the best!" Gina hugged everybody in the room.

"Thank Humble and Kienna, they set this up for you." GG made it known to her.

"Thank you so much, Humble. I'm sorry again for everything that happened and I really think you are a good match for my best."

"No thanks needed, Munchie. Whatever I can do to make you happy, sis. You had it rough these last few months, so it's all good." Humble spoke, candidly.

"That's still no way for me to act."

"Okay, now that this *Leave It To Beaver* ass moment is over, one of yo' gifts is in the back, Munchie." Gallardo called out and handed her a small box.

"Oooohhh, big brother, what did you get me?" Gina was jumping up and down, full of excitement and wonder.

"Yo' father bought you this. Getcho ass back there and see!"

"Ughhhh, you're so rude!" Gina playfully rolled her eyes and ran to the back to see what it was.

When Gina made it out of the studio's back door, her jaw was almost to the floor. Wrapped in a bow, sat an all black 2017 Jeep Sahara. It was the one she wanted for the longest. This was truly a great moment for her. Gina tore the key fob out of the gift box that

Gallardo gave her. She ran over to her truck, so she could play with the controls and everything.

After she played with it for a few, Gina came back into the studio and ate the food that Kienna's cousin, Germany cooked for the kick-back. It was an array of food spread out on two tables. There was BBQ meatballs, three cheese macaroni, tacos, buffalo wings, fried shrimp, homemade mango peach salsa and guacamole, tortilla chips, Rotel dip, and some burgers with cheese and there were a selections of toppings and condiments on the table.

As she was eating, Serry and Allure walked into the studio. In the last few months, she had developed a crush on him. Serry was dope as hell and even though he was rude as shit, she valued their friend-ship. Serry was holding a gift bag that was in her favorite color: mint green.

Gina found herself lusting after him. He was wearing a white Gucci button up that was open and showed off his well-defined chest with all of the tattoos on it, a pair of red Gucci jogger shorts that showed off that immaculate print he had between his legs, and a pair of the Ferrari Jordan 14's on his feet. His hair wasn't wild as it usually was. He had it braided into two braids going to his back. His beard was on point as well. Gina couldn't stare too hard because she didn't want her brother to be mad at her again. They just recently started back talking. Gallardo took her not telling him about Burnah pretty hard. Speaking of Burnah, he was the only one that wasn't at the party. Gina hadn't seen him much since she threw the food at him. She knew he was still working with the fellas, but keeping his distance from her. She would be a damn lie if she said that she didn't still love him, but Gina knew that things would never work out with them.

"Hey, Serry! Hey, Allure." She hugged both of them.

"Wassup, sis. Here's yo' gift! A nigga just came to grub for real. Happy Birthday to you, though." Allure replied and walked away to go get some of the food that was on the tables.

Allure left her and Serry standing there.

"Here go yo' gift, Munchie." Serry handed her the bag.

"Thank you so much."

"You know it's all love. Let me go holla at my niggas. Happy Birthday with yo' little sexy ass." He replied and gave her a wink.

Gina couldn't help, but blush. She snapped out of it and added Serry's gifts to the others.

She made her way to the food and enjoyed herself with her family and friends. This was one of her best birthdays ever. Gina couldn't even complain about the turn of events. Her family had busy schedules, but made it a point to spend her special day with her.

ƐƐƐƐƐƐƐ

After all of the festivities, Gina headed home in her new Jeep and Gallardo drove her old Toyota Camry to their mother's house in Baldwin Hills. They made it to her house and Gallardo helped her place the gifts and her birthday cake in the house. After speaking to his mother, Gallardo left out of the house.

Gina went to her room and sat on the bed. She decided to open Serry's gift first. When she looked in the bag, however, there were several gifts inside.

The first thing that she dug into was the card. It was a hand-written one.

MUNCH,

A nigga ain't good at shit like this, but Happy Birthday. Hope yo' shit is dope and you like this shit I picked up. I wanna take yo' ass to dinner next week too, so free up some time.

-SERRY

She opened the wrapping off of all of the gifts. In total there were four. There was a pair of olive Fenty slides, the mint green Nike Huraches she wanted, a matching Nike shirt, some Twizzlers, and a front row ticket for her to see Rihanna in concert. It wasn't really about what he gave her, it was more of the fact that he listened. They talked on the phone almost everyday and were developing a friendship. Serry was rude and rough around the edges, but he was so sweet to her. He had her really thinking about the possibility of trying to give him a chance.

21

BURNAH

*A*fter the whole Gina situation and what Gallardo did to him on the block, Burnah decided it was best for him to lay low away from the crew. He didn't want to beef with one of his niggas over a bitch. Even if that bitch was his sister. In retrospect, he was dead ass wrong for even pursuing something with Gina. He knew that he wasn't shit, but still wanted to be selfish. Burnah was one of those niggas who wanted their cake and to eat it too. He would still be ducking with other hoes, even if he was supposed to be in a committed relationship. That's just how he was built. His mother made him feel like all women were weak and not to be trusted. He felt like he needed to play them before they played him. He saw them as toys. He would play for a while, but wouldn't hesitate to put you on the shelf if something else more exciting and better came along.

For now, he had been sticking with Tasha, the nurse that was sucking his dick in the hospital room. She had some fire head and grade A pussy. That was all Burnah needed from a woman, so she was serving her purpose, for now. They had been fucking around on the low. He hadn't heard anything from Gina, so he took his frustrations out on Tasha's pussy. She didn't mind because she loved the rough shit.

"Damn, that shit was good, as usual." Burnah was trying to catch his breath after another fucking session with Tasha.

"I aim to please, Daddy." Tasha responded, reaching over to the nightstand to grab the BIC lighter and the half of joint of Green Crack and cocaine mix from the ashtray.

They were already high, but she wanted to be higher. Burnah rose up from the bed and ripped the condom from his dick, so he could dispose of it in the bathroom. He didn't trust women and wouldn't be caught slipping if he had anything to do with it. Tasha was only a temporary fix to deal with the hurt that Burnah felt like Gina caused him. It's crazy that she ended their thing when they weren't even together. He didn't understand why he couldn't fuck other females. Gina couldn't fuck other niggas, but that was besides the point.

Burnah washed his hands and walked back in the room and laid across the bed. Tasha was inhaling the weed smoke and staring at him. He found that to be really sexy. Gina would smoke with him, but he felt like she was too prissy for it. Tasha had sex appeal written all over her. From the blonde twenty-inch bundles in her head, to her perfectly arched eyebrows, her almond colored skin, that sneaky smile she has, and her body that could easily put Rita Ora or Melyssa Ford out of business. She was nothing like Gina. She was raised out on Slauson Ave with that extra side of larceny in her heart.

"Ay, get up and get yo ass dressed. A nigga want some *Roscoe's*." Burnah called out, rising from the bed to find something to wear.

€€€€€€€

Thirty minutes later, Burnah was pulling up into the parking lot of Roscoe's. He got out of the car and Tasha followed behind him in the short ass shorts, crop top, and heels she was wearing. Burnah walked in and they stood in line. As he was typing into his phone, he heard a familiar laugh. It kind of made his heartbeat speed up. He hadn't seen Gina in a while. Hearing her laugh, made him realize how much he missed her. Glancing behind him at the tables, made his blood boil. Gina was sitting there with Serry, laughing like shit was gravy. He wanted to choke her ass up, but decided against it. He had never liked Serry and now this was another thing to add to the list.

Before he could control himself, Burnah was walking briskly, over to their table. He had no emotion on his face, whatsoever.

"Oh, you can be all in this restaurant laughing, but can't return my calls and texts!"

"I don't want to talk to you, so I blocked your number. Now, if you would excuse me, I was eating my dinner in peace," Gina resumed her conversation with Serry.

"See, you got me fucked up, bitch! You in here being a hoe with this bitch made nigga and think I'm about to go for that! Hell the fuck naw!" Burnah voice boomed through the restaurant.

People were watching and it got really quiet. Serry stood up from his seat and walked over to where Burnah was standing.

"Ay, I don't know what the fuck yo' problem is, but you ain't about to be in this bitch acting like I got hoe in my blood." Serry stated, calmly.

"Fuck out of here. You ain't nothing, but Humble's bitch. Get the fuck outta my face! This between me and my bitch!" The effects of the cocaine and weed were making Burnah erratic.

"Fuck you, Burnah. Get yo purse and shit, Munchie...we about to go." Serry told her, still looking at Burnah in the eye.

Tasha walked over and stood next to Burnah.

"How are you in here causing a scene and you're in here with the same bitch I saw you with in the hospital."

"You know what it is with that stanking bitch. I don't love that hoe." Burnah replied, starting to sweat and spittle was coming from his mouth.

"You don't love me either, so fuck you!" Gina snapped, slapping him in the face.

On reflex, Burnah punched her in the mouth, causing her jaw to shift and bleed.

Serry saw red and jumped straight on Burnah, sending blows to his face and body. Gina was on the ground holding her face, obviously hurting from the blow. She pulled out her phone and called Tress and her sister. She knew if she called Gallardo at that moment, things would be bigger than they already were.

Burnah laid on the floor, unconscious and she was sure that the manager called the *LAPD* by now. Serry helped her up and carried her bridal-style out of *Roscoe's*.

22

TRESS

"*D*amn, you are so fucking sexy anytime of the day," Tress complimented Gretchen as she laid in his arms.

They both managed to get up at the same time. Tress wanted to take Gretchen to meet his grandparents and siblings. It was a long time coming for the meeting. He had told each the other, but now was the time that they could put a face to the woman. Tress was lowkey excited, but scared as well. He knew if his grandmother didn't like GG, then their relationship would never work. That was just how much his Mameux and Pappadeux meant to him.

Tress rose out of the bed and stretched his body a few times. GG admired his body as he stood there, naked as the day as he was brought in his world. His dick was standing at attention, showing off that morning wood.

"Like something you see?" Tress arched his eyebrows, in curiosity.

"Definitely." Gretchen replied, sauntering over to him, squinting her eyes at him, sexily.

Tress picked her up and she immediately wrapped her legs around his waist. Without warning, he entered her ocean. They both let out collective moans and GG rode his dick, mid-air. She loved that Tress could pick her up and just get it in. It made the sex more exciting. He pulled out of her and lifted her up like an accordion and started eating her pussy.

"Uhmmmm don't stop! Damn, Tresssss!" She moaned, loudly as she ran her hands through his low, curly mane.

He wasn't wearing it in his usual Dutch braids. She took them out the day before and washed his hair. It didn't matter that he came in at midnight from doing Black Heart Militia business, she stayed up and waited for him. She was basically staying with Tress.

He couldn't sleep without being inside her or her being near him. Tress continued his oral assault on her southern lips and walls. GG turned upside down and took his hard shaft in her mouth.

"Fuckkkkk, girllll!" Tress almost dropped her from the impact her jaws had on his dick.

It felt so good and he loved how freaky Gretchen was. She made sure he was satisfied just like how he made her feel. Not able to take the pressure of her mouth anymore, Tress picked her up and placed her back on his dick. He moved to a wall and placed her back against it. He stared at her as he stabbed his dick in her. Gretchen had her eyes closed.

"Shit, this dick is so fucking good!"

"Who...stroke...dick...stroke...is this?" Tress asked, in between long stroking her.

"Shit, it's mine, nigga! You're fucking the shit out of Zaddy's pussy! I'm about to cummmmmm!"

"Splash that juice on this dick. Daddy's waiting!" Tress groaner in her ear.

"Here it come!"

"I'm about to nut, too! Fuck ! I can't hold it!" They climaxed together and engaged in a deep tongue kiss.

Catching their breaths, they were just frozen, in the same spot. Tress didn't even want to move, but he didn't want his weight to crush GG.

Tress placed her down on wobbly legs and they headed to the shower. They needed to hurry up. They were meeting Tress' family at his grandparents' house for brunch.

€€€€€€€

They sat in the car, in traffic. Tress looked over and saw Gretchen looking out of the window. She was so beautiful to him. He could feel her palm sweating, so he knew she was nervous. He took her hand that was in his and kissed it. That got her attention.

"You good?" Tress asked, concerned for her.

"What if your grandparents and siblings don't like me? Then what?"

"They will love you. You make me happy and to know you is to love you, baby.

"I hope so." Gretchen gave him a wry smile.

They listened to music and sang along, until the traffic died down. They rode for a few more minutes and arrived at a nice two-story house on Alondra Ave. Tress parked on the side and waited for a car to go past. He hopped out of the car and went over to Gretchen's side to open her door. Once they opened the gate and walked up to the porch, Tress fished his keys out of his pocket and opened the door. The fresh smell of fried chicken and pancakes permeated the air. Tress was ready to dig in the food. His grandmother could cook her ass off.

"Ay, I'm here. Where y'all at?"

"Tresshaun Alexander Stephens, you better stop yelling in my house." His grandmother called him by his government name, eliciting laughter from GG.

"My bad, Mameux!" He apologized.

"That's what I thought. Who is this little chocolate drop here?" Audrey inquired about Gretchen.

"This is my girlfriend, Gretchen Miller." Tress introduced her, proudly.

"Nice to meet you, ma'am. Tresshaun has told me so much about you." Gretchen smiled at her.

"Nice to meet you too, beautiful. Call me Mameux, like this fool and his siblings do."

"Thanks, Mameux."

"Okay, well the rest of them are waiting for y'all at the table. Let's get going." Tress and Gretchen followed behind his grandmother.

They entered the dining room and Tress introduced Gretchen to everyone else in the room. They all liked her and started to dig into the food on the table. It was a great spread. His grandmother made fried chicken, macaroni and cheese, waffles, collard greens, and yams. She also made pound cake and banana pudding for dessert. Tress and Gretchen knew they would have to double time in the gym to work all of that food.

They ended up staying at his grandparents' house all day long, watching TV, looking through old family photos, and playing *Call of Duty* on Trayden's PS4. The only one who didn't play was Tristan. She retired upstairs because she had to get ready for work. After saying their goodbyes and promising to come over the next week, Tress and Gretchen left from the house. They got back in the car and just sat there for a second.

"Told you that you didn't have anything to worry about. My folks love you."

"I see that. Your Mameux cooked her ass off. That food was so good!" Gretchen yelped, excitedly.

"I know yo' greedy ass loved it." Tress poked fun of her.

"Fuck you!" She shot up her middle finger.

"That can be arranged when we get home..shit, I'll fuck you on the shoulder of the highway."

"You are so damn nasty." Gretchen moaned, anticipating his superb dick game.

"You know that I'm nasty." Tress smiled and licked his lips.

"Whatever."

Gretchen's phone rang and it was connected to the system of Tress' Tahoe. It was her sister, Gina calling. Last she heard, Serry was picking her up from school and they were going to have dinner.

She answered the phone on the second ring.

"Hello?"

"Ay, this Serry...you around the big homie, Tress?" He asked, sounding like he was pissed.

"Yes...what's wrong? Where is my sister, Serry?"

"That fuck nigga, Burnah punched her in the mouth and her jaw may be broken. We're at *UCLA*

Medical."

"We're on the way!" Gretchen yelled and hung up the phone.

"Everything will be okay, baby. I will get you there." Tress cranked the truck up and flew up the block, like a bat out of hell.

23

GG

*G*retchen sat in the emergency room and Serry ran the story back to them. She never liked Burnah and this solidified it for her. She couldn't believe that he hit her sister in the mouth like that. The shit had her thrown for a loop. She paced the waiting room as they waited for word on Gina's condition. She didn't want to call Gallardo or Zip, but knew that she had to. That was just a disaster just waiting to happen. Those two were very overprotective of Gina. She was the youngest in their family and would click if something happened to her. They definitely were about to lose their shit.

After calling her mother, Gallardo, and Zip, Gretchen went to go sit with Tress. He rubbed her shoulders and tried to console her. The doctors hadn't come to give them any updates, so they just waited.

"Baby, things will be alright," Tress places a kiss on GG's shoulder and then on her lips.

"I hope so. That's my little sister, my baby." The tears were falling from her face and she was stressing herself out from thinking the worst.

"WHERE THE FUCK IS MY SISTER?" Gretchen rose up quickly when she heard her brother's raised voice.

Gallardo was dressed in all black and his eyes were just as dark as his attire. She feared that his temper would get him in trouble. Zip was right behind him, with Suri holding Zasaya in her arms. They still hadn't heard much from Saya, so Zip was the only parent she had, for now.

Gretchen walked over to them to try and calm them down.

"G, you gotta calm down. They won't hesitate to put ya ass in jail." She chastised him.

"Fuck this shit! I asked that bald headed bitch with them run over shoes what the fuck was going on with my sister. She better tell me something 'fore her teeth be on the ground. I don't give a fuck right now."

"What the fuck happened to Munchie, GG?" Zip directed his question to her.

"I don't know much, except for what Serry told me. You would have to ask him."

"Fuck!" Zip hollered out.

"You all will have to calm down or I'll have to get security to escort you all out.

"Take yo' ugly, four eyed ass on somewhere. Fuck out of here!" Serry yelled out, letting his temper get the best of him.

Seeing that things were about to escalate, Gretchen intervened in the exchange.

"You don't have to kick us out. We will chill." She responded and the lady walked away.

€€€€€€€

After Gina, GG, and Gallardo's mother showed up, they all calmed down. All of them knew that Serita Miller was not with the shits. She wouldn't hesitate to backhand any of them like they were a hoe on *Sunset Boulevard*. OD was the nigga to fear in Compton, but his wife was the queen of enforcing that fear. Her little short ass didn't mess around. Serita was able to find out that Gina was in surgery. The doctors would be out to speak to her when the surgery was finished.

"Look, Mrs. Serita, I respect you and all, but this shit is fucked up. On me, imma find that nigga." Serry was so angry that he was pacing around the waiting room.

They were in one of the family waiting rooms and it was only all of them in there.

"I know you do, which is why imma let all that cursing and shit ride. Now, until we figure out what is wrong with my youngest baby, none of y'all niggas are leaving this hospital. Now, this time is about Gina. The rest of that shit is irrelevant. Understand?" She directed her statement to everyone in the room.

"Yes ma'am."

They all shut up and waited for the doctor to come and speak to them. GG was so tired that she found herself falling asleep on Tress' shoulder. He picked her up and laid her across his massive chest. She looked like a little rag doll on his big, muscular body. She felt safe in his arms. She loved being under Tress. He was her stress reliever and Lord knows she was stressed as hell at this time.

Some time must have went by because GG didn't wake up, until she felt Tress rise up and pick her up like she was a baby. Her eyes fluttered open and two doctors and Nikayla were headed their way.

"Are you all the family of Gina Miller?" The first doctor inquired, looking at all of them.

Gretchen went to go stand next to her mother. She hoped they were given great news because were looking grim.

"Yes, I'm her mother." Their mother spoke, as Gallardo held one of her hands and GG the other.

The doctor was a black man and he appeared to maybe be in his thirties, had long dreads that were wrapped in an Oakland Raiders head wrapping, light brown eyes, and appeared as if he worked out. He didn't look like your typical doctor.

"I'm Dr. Paige and this is my colleague, Dr. Steinbeck. I am the surgeon that worked on your daughter. Dr. Steinbeck is the orthopedic surgeon on call. Ma'am, Gina had successful surgeries, however, her jaw was broken in two places and we had to remove three teeth because they cut into her cheek. We had place screws and wires in her mouth to fix the dislocation. Her arm was fractured in three places and will need physical therapy. She also had a small laceration on her head and a mild concussion." Dr. Paige explained, in laymen's terms. He didn't use the usual doctor jargon, which they were all thankful for.

"Can we see her?" Their mom asked.

"Yes, you can. We're having her placed in a room as we speak. Dr. Steinbeck will explain to you about what kind of care she will need. After that, Nurse Nikayla will show you all where Ms. Miller's room is. You all have a nice night and I will keep her in my prayers."

"Thank you, Dr. Paige for all you have done." Their mom thanked him.

"No thanks needed, ma'am. I'm just doing my job." Dr. Paige trotted away, leaving them in the waiting room.

"Hi, Ms. Miller will have to undergo speech therapy and physical therapy. Her jaw should heal in six to eight weeks. Her arm may take eight to ten. She suffered fractures to some pretty important and vital bones in her body. She will be under an extensive amount of pain meds to alleviate the pain. She's lucky to have a support system like this one here...she will need it. Thank you all. Have a wonderful night." Gallardo shook his hand and he was on his way.

Nikayla looked at Gallardo and knew he probably was going to be out for blood. She couldn't do much to console him while she was on the clock.

"Are y'all okay?" She directed her question to Gallardo, Gretchen, and their mother.

"We are okay, sweetie. My God spared my baby. It could have been worse than this." Their mother replied, with a small smile.

"Ay, I'm about to get out of here. I can't find this nigga in this hospital. Black Mask Militia, we out." Gallardo commanded, causing all of them to rise up.

Tress kissed Gretchen on the lips and they stared into each other's eyes for a second.

"Be careful."

"I will be. Gotta make sure bruh don't be on no wild shit— I mean stuff...sorry, Mrs. Serita."

"It's okay. Just look out for my bullheaded son."

"Yes ma'am." Tress left out of the automatic glass doors of the hospital to catch up with his crew.

"I like him for you." Gretchen's mother told her.

"Me too." She agreed, with a smile.

Gretchen's mother tapped her on the knee and rose up to meet Nikayla at the doors leading to the hospital rooms.

Gretchen sent up a small prayer for Tress and Gallardo. Nikayla rounded them up to go see Gina. GG hoped that all of them came back in one piece, but she knew that Burnah had written his own death certificate when he decided to put his hands on her sister.

24

THAILAND

*B*eing back on the east coast made Thai realize just how much she missed home and her family. It was something about New York and New Jersey that awakened her. She still loved Philly as well, but hadn't been back since her parents cut her off. The only ones they had left were the twins. Thai used to have a strong relationship with them, but couldn't bring herself to talk to them now.

Thai hadn't heard from KB since he left her brother, Henré's house. She still couldn't believe that he and Buddah had come to blows at her niece's birthday party. Neither Buddah or Buck would talk to her since they knew she was pregnant. Once it was revealed, she was so shocked that KB knew. She also wanted to know how he found out. Only person she told was her sister in law, Adreena and she swore her to secrecy.

Thai sat in Adreena's living room with the ladies as they had a movie night/sleepover. They were all wearing onesies. Adreena kicked Banks, Adrian, and baby B out of the house. He didn't mind going over to stay the night with one of his brothers. Bailey and Banks were the only ones that weren't tripping about Thai having a child and a man in her life. Henré had mixed feelings and was kind of siding with Buck and Buddah. She other ladies were drinking Pink Moscato, while she sipped on sparkling grape juice. This was cheering her up and she was thankful.

"Cheer up, darling. Your brothers will come around. We were all shocked to find out your little ass was pregnant. That KB is a rude mothefucker. He remind me so much of Buddah." Mona replied, filling her plate up with meatballs and macaroni and cheese.

"Yeah, I know. His ass is crazy too. It's like almost all LA niggas are psycho. His boys are no exception." Thai let out a sigh.

"They can't be as worse as these NY and Jersey niggas. Can they?" Briia questioned, with a serious expression.

"They definitely are." Thailand answered, matter-of-factly.

"Damn!" All of them responded, in unison.

€€€€€€€

Once everyone was sleep, Thailand was still up. She sat in the windowsill in the living room and just looked at the luminous stars and the moon. For some reason, she was missing KB and her hand went to her stomach. She was growing a real baby in there and barely knew her child's father. It scared and excited her at the same time. As she was deep in thought, her iPhone vibrated against the perch of the windowsill. Thailand picked it up and it was KB FaceTiming her. She accepted the call.

"What is it that you want, Kashim?"

"Why you got that lil funky ass attitude. I should be the one mad. Ya really wasn't going to tell a nigga yo' ass was pregnant?"

"How did you find that out?" She inquired, looking at him seriously.

"I have my ways. So, how is my baby in there? I didn't call for yo' big head ass."

"Whatever. I'm fine...thanks for asking." She responded, sarcasm evident in her voice.

"Still don't believe I asked yo' spider monkey looking ass how you was. I was talking to my princess in there." KB frowned his face up at her.

"I can't stand you, ugh!"

"You know you lowkey love me, baby mama."

"Shiddddd!" Thailand called out, causing both of them to laugh.

"Baby mama, I'm glad I called ya...man yo' ass cheering me up for real." KB let out an exasperated sigh.

"What's wrong, Kashim?" Thai asked, her voices full of concern.

"Burnah broke Munchie's jaw and arm the other night. She had to get like twenty something stitches and arm in a cast. All of us been combing the streets looking for this bitch made nigga. Never knew one of my niggas could turn pussy like that. Shit is crazy to me."

"Ohmigosh! That's crazy."

"Tell me about it. Well, I was just calling yo' ass to see wassup. I gotta go." KB said his goodbye and ended the FaceTime call.

Thai rose from the windowsill and went to lie back on the sectional. She needed to get some sleep and was glad that KB called her. She couldn't handle that her brothers weren't talking to her, but it was something about KB's rude ass that she liked.

25

NIKAYLA

*G*allardo has been going through so much, dealing with what happened to his sister and all of his Black Mask Militia business that Nikayla wanted to do something special for him. He wanted no one to make a big deal out of his twenty-fifth birthday, so Nikayla decided to take him to Miami. He needed to get away for some time to get his mind together.

He had been in the streets more and drinking, heavily. She knew it had something to do with his visit with his dad and having the daunting tasks of having to kill one of his best friends. All she wanted to do was be his ride-or-die because Gallardo needed Nikayla now, more than ever. Since this particular day was one of his "off days" Nikayla decided to wake him up, properly. She slowly moved the covers back and was face to face with Gallardo's dick, straining against the Champion shorts he was wearing. He didn't wear underwear, but did put on some shorts. Most nights, Nikayla and Naheem spent the night and he would climb in the bed with them. Fortunately for them, he stayed in his room.

She untied the waistband of his shorts and pulled them down. Looking up, she was staring into his eyes. Gallardo was a light sleeper, so he woke up. He took his hand and guided Nikayla's mouth slowly down the length of his substantial size dick. She sucked on the head as if it was a pacifier, garnering moans and groans from him.

"Fuccckkk! You sucking this dick like you want me to claim you on my income tax."

He didn't just say that, did he? Nikayla asked herself, fighting the urge to laugh her ass off.

"Damn, bae, this head is superb, top of the line." Gallardo confessed, in a pleasure-induced haze.

His toes were curling and his eyes were in slits. Nikayla smiled on the inside as she got the reaction that she set out to get. She loved to see the faces he made when she swallowed him whole and didn't gag.

"Shittttt! A nigga about to bust a big nut! Ahhhhhh!" Gallardo hollered out, releasing his kids into her awaiting mouth.

She swallowed it with no hesitation. Afterwards, she slid up to meet his lips. They engaged in a sloppy tongue kiss and Gallardo entered her, sliding his whole dick inside. They looked into each other's eyes as Nikayla slowly rode him. She loved being in control and by the slits in his eyes, Gallardo was well satisfied each time. Speeding up her strokes, it was getting too good to her. Gallardo started stroking her from below.

"Shitttt! Galllllaaarrrdddoo! I'm coming! Fuck me harder, babe!" She yelled out, as he started to gain the control.

Gallardo turned her over with his dick still inside. He looked down and saw how Nikayla had creamed all over his dick. She was enjoying this dick down.

"Cum again for me, Nik Nik." Gallardo whispered, against her ear.

They were sweating and he was on the brink of cumming, as well. They both wanted to outfuck the other one. That's just how they were whenever they had sex. A few strokes later and they were climaxing together.

After showering and completing their third round, Gallardo had to leave to go handle his street business and Nikayla decided to clean up the house. She started with the back of the house and worked her way up to the front, she saw Naheem and Serry playing Call of Duty.

"Hey, Naheem and Serry." She spoke to them on her way to the kitchen.

They just waved and continued to play the game. Nikayla chuckled and went about her business. She had plenty of time to take care of home before they left for their flight later that night. She got ahold of her cousin, Torren and he gave her his private plane to utilize. They hadn't talked in years, but he was willing to do that favor for her. At one point, he was trying to get her to move to the Middle East, but she wasn't about that life or didn't want to uproot Naheem. They already had a tough time when Nathan died.

Later that night...

"Baby, where are we going?" Gallardo inquired, as he sat in the passenger seat of Nikayla's Hyundai Equus. He was smoking a freshly rolled joint and relaxing for a change. These past few weeks he had been moving like crazy. In between meetings, meeting the plug out of town, combing the streets for Burnah and being heads on with the street and legal businesses. He hadn't had much time to sit down and take a breather.

"Just wait and see. I promise you will love it. It's just me showing you my appreciation."

"Okay. I'll sit back." He smiled and kept smoking his bud.

Nikayla stole glances at him and felt her lady parts juicing up in response. It took Gallardo little effort to have her feeling like her pussy was gushing like a waterfall. He was fine as hell and all hers. Them eyes of his made her go crazy, too. She saw other bitches staring, but he paid them no mind.

They arrived at the private sector of LAX and Nikayla parked near the hangar. Her uncle, Danye was standing at the hangar waiting on them. Nikayla ran until she was in his arms.

"akhw al'umi! akhw al'umi!" She yelled uncle, in her native tongue.

Gallardo stood off to the side and just smiled at the interaction. Nikayla and Danye walked over to the car.

"Hey, Heavy, heard so much about you. I haven't seen this girl smile like this in a while. Thank you."

"No thanks needed. She does the same for me." Gallardo replied, truthfully.

"Well, I want to get you guys out to Charlotte, where I'm staying when I'm not in the Middle East. Sounds good to you all?"

"Yeah, that's wassup." Gallardo replied, with a smile.

They talked to Danye for a little bit more and then they boarded the private plane.

"Damn, ya plugged in for real. Why ya don't talk about this side of yo' family?"

"They didn't really approve of me being with Nathan...they didn't honestly start talking back with me, until my dad died. Other than that I didn't hear from them. Plus, I didn't want to be involved in that life. Ya know?"

"I feel ya, ma. So, where we going? Yo' ass didn't let a nigga pack anything."

"I packed it for you. Sit back and enjoy the ride." Nikayla kissed him on the lips and he smacked her on the ass.

€€€€€€€€

The next afternoon...

After spending most of the morning in the bed, Gallardo and Nikayla finally came up for air. They decided to hit up the Aventura Mall to shop. Nikayla was happy that Gallardo was enjoying himself and not letting what happened in LA, consume him. He was smiling and being free. Sometimes a person needs a stress reliever.

They held hands as they walked through the mall shopping in Gucci, Prada, Nike, and some other places along the way. They made three trips to the rental car. Nikayla tried to foot the bill on things, but Gallardo passed her three wads of cash and told her to go dumb. They both bought so much stuff for themselves, Naheem, and their people back home. They even went inside of the arcade and played around. The sun was going down, so they ended up on the beach, to enjoy the rest of the day.

Nikayla was wearing a Puma short set, but under it, she wore this distressed bathing suit that her high school friend, Coral made. She had her own clothing line called, C. Rave. Nikayla bought several pieces from her for this trip and just to wear, in general. She supported her friends' dreams. Gallardo couldn't keep his hands off of her as they sat in the cabana he rented out for them.

"Damn, this bathing suit make you look sexy as fuck!" He complimented, licking them big, juicy lips of his.

"Thank you, babe." She blushed and sipped on the Blood Orange Mike's Hard Lemonade, she was grasping in her hand.

"You fine as fuck, so—," Gallardo's voice trailed off and he started looking in the direction of the water.

Nikayla trained her eye to his line of vision and there stood Burnah, acting as if he didn't just assault Gina a few weeks prior. He was living up, with some woman. Gallardo remained quiet as they sat there to wait for Burnah to leave. She knew it was about to be some shit.

HEAVY

*H*eavy stood in the spot he was in and watched Burnah living it up, in deep disgust. He couldn't believe that all this time he was looking for him that he was on the other side of the country. In this moment, he was not Gallardo, he was transforming into Heavy. He couldn't do anything to Burnah because he had no guns or anything. He could beat him with his bare hands, but that would be too easy. He was going to call the crew when he got back to the hotel.

Himself and Nikayla sat inside of the cabana until the sun went down. They headed to the other side of the strip to get to their hotel. After shopping, they headed back to the hotel and changed clothes. Instead of driving to the beach, they decided to walk the strip. He was deep in thoughts as they headed back to the hotel. They were staying in The *Setai, Miami Beach*. He was so deep in his thoughts and Nikayla was looking in her phone. The sound of a gun cocking got his attention.

"Give me yo' shit or you and your girl's brains will be on the ground.

Gallardo started laughing because I couldn't believe that he was adding being robbed to the list of problems he had.

"So, is this the part where I'm supposed to surrender and give ya my shit?" Gallardo caught the robber by surprise.

Nikayla was stunned into silence. She was scared as hell, Gallardo could see it in her eyes. That pissed him off more than anything.

"I'm the one with the gun...stop fucking with me before I pull this trigger," the robber hollered, but he had a little shakiness in his voice.

Gallardo turned around and looked at who was holding him at gunpoint. He knew that he was a teenager. He took in his appearance. The kid was like six feet tall, he was wearing all black, but Gallardo could tell that he was homeless. The all black Air Force 1s were coming apart, his black Levi's were faded and had better days, the black V-neck he wore had s few holes in it. He had on one of those face shields and the gun in his hand was rusty. He reminded Gallardo of Humble.

"You done yet, lil nigga. That shit ain't even loaded. Fuck outta here." Gallardo took his fist and connected it to the young boy's face.

He was going to spare his life because he could see that the young man was down on his luck. He was just going to beat the shit out of him. Gallardo was dressed in swimming trunks and flip flops. He punched the young man around a few more times and then helped him up.

"Ow! Fuckkkk!" The young boy yelled as he removed the face shield.

He spit out blood on the ground and looked up at Gallardo and Nikayla, in deep embarrassment.

"Lil nigga, what's your name?"

"Khaleem," The young boy replied, in his signature deep voice.

He was still spitting out blood and was in some pain. Nikayla kept her mouth closed, but now that she saw her man handling things, she wasn't frightened anymore.

"Khaleem, bring yo' ass." Gallardo replied, simply as he took Nikayla's hand in his and made his way to the hotel.

A few hours later...

Gallardo and Khaleem rode around the rental to Miami International Airport. The crew was arriving via the private. Gallardo would have to show Nikayla's people his gratitude, soon. This plane came in handy with keeping them under the radar. They had secret compartments for weapons and all. That concealment was needed for them.

"So, what's your story, lil nigga? Why yo' ass out here playing with yo' life? I could've easily kill ya with no remorse."

"I've been taking care of myself since I was twelve...only way for me to survive." Khaleem shrugged, wincing from the ill-fitting Air Forces on his feet.

"Where yo' people at?"

"My mama died from a drug overdose and my auntie too busy chasing niggas to take care of me. My dad in the Feds for the next twenty years." Khaleem replied, like he was tired of telling the story.

"Aight. I gotcha."

"Why you being nice to me? I had a gun to the back of your head?" Khaleem was confused at all of the niceties that Gallardo was showing him.

"I can see ya a good kid. Lil nigga, I could've easily killed ya ass. I'm not from here, so I had to call back a little. If you ever point a gun at me or my girl again, I will kill you...no hesitation." Gallardo stared at him, intensely, wanting him to see the seriousness in this situation.

"I got it." The rest of the ride was silent.

Gallardo's thoughts were back to the fact that he was about to kill Burnah. This Miami trio proved to be a great thing for the crew.

Zip, Tress, Humble and KB all walked off of the plane and got into the two Yukon Denalis that he had Nikayla rent for this event. Due to his immense connections, his connect allowed them to use his warehouse and the house he owned near the beach. Gallardo dapped his niggas up and they loaded into the vehicles to head to the house.

Once they made it into the house, the ball could start rolling.

"I called y'all niggas because a nigga on vacation and came across Burnah. Nigga is here in Miami and it's time we put in that murder game."

"Damn, we been looking for that nigga everywhere and he

booked it to Miami. Pussy ass nigga," Zip spat, still mad that his cousin had to go through that ordeal.

"My sentiments, exactly." Gallardo replied.

"So, you know where the nigga at?" Tress inquired, cracking his knuckles.

"Yeah, Enrikqto and his people came through."

"Well, you know we down to help you with that homicide." Humble referred to himself and every other man in the car.

"I'm just ready for that fuck nigga to die." KB replied, in his typical nonchalant manner.

"Oh yeah, this is Khaleem. Khaleem, this my niggas. I'm bringing him back to LA when we go back."

"That's wassup." They all replied.

After squaring off the details, Gallardo and Khaleem left the men to do whatever. The house had seven bedrooms, so they were good. They would be killing Burnah in the next two days. In those two days, Gallardo was going to spend time with Nikayla and get to know Khaleem.

27

BURNAH

*L*ooking over his shoulder and being on high alert was not how Burnah wanted to spend his life. He knew after beating the hell out of Gina that Gallardo would be looking for him. With the help of one of his homies, he was able to relocate to Miami. Since being there, he didn't feel as unsafe as he did in Los Angeles. Out there, he felt like he had a target on his back. He knew how Gallardo got down, so he was aware that he would die whenever he caught up with him. Laid up in a seedy hotel near the beach, he spent most of his nights in the club or getting high. He was hooked to the cocaine and didn't see himself putting it down anytime soon. He didn't look at himself in the mirror these days because he knew he was a junkie just like his mother. He also knew that if he wasn't under the influence of that nose candy, shit wouldn't have went left with him and Gina the way that it did. He missed him Munchie and it enraged him when he thought that maybe she was entertaining Serry. He never liked him and there wasn't even a reason.

Snnniiffff!!!!

Burnah took a very long line of nose candy and then dipped vodka on his nose. He was already high as hell, but he needed the stamina to keep being able to have sex with one of the strippers from

King of Diamonds. He finessed Passion off of their addiction being something that they had in common. They had been fucking and snorting for hours. They were sweating and the air conditioner in the hotel room was on full blast. The headboard was hitting against the bed, violently as the sounds of Tank blared from Passion's cellphone. The noise was to the point where the hotel could kick them out for disregarding ordinances. After a few more strokes, Burnah nutted into the condom. He was a little winded, but played it off.

"Damn, that pussy is phenomenal!" He complimented Passion on her sexual prowess.

"I aim to please, baby. I'm about to hop in the shower. I have to work the day and night shift at the club.

Passion rose her naked body from the bed and headed to the bathroom. Burnah's eyes were on her body. He was lowkey hypnotized. Once Passion made it to the bathroom, Burnah laid his head back and took a small little nap.

After eating some *Johnny Rockets* for lunch and drinking a few daiquiris from Wet Willies, Burnah was walking Miami Beach with not a care in the world. The girl was next to him. He didn't even know her name, but she was going to be his victim that night. Unbeknownst to him, his life was hanging in the balance. He wasn't paying attention to his surroundings, so it was easy for him to be caught slipping. He was still very much high, so he was careless even in his state of paranoia.

Waking up to a burst of cold water hitting his body, Burnah came face to face to the cold and uncaring eyes of Gallardo. Zip, Tress, Humble, and KB stood behind him. Burnah gulped, in fear. He knew he was looking death right in the eyes. There was no way in Hell that he was walking away from this, alive.

He just took a deep breath and accepted his fate. It was crazy that his life was hanging in the balance, but he had no one to blame for himself. All the crazy shit he did to Gina while under the influence of the coke was unnecessary, but it was too late to turn back the hands of time. He was losing his life.

28

MUNCHIE

Since getting home from the hospital, Gina had been depressed and not wanting to do anything. She felt so disgusted in herself that she didn't see this coming from Burnah. He really had the wool over her eyes. How could he beat her down like that? This was a man that she loved and he just messed her over like she was yesterday's trash. What pissed her off the most was that she strained the relationship between herself and her siblings for a fuckboy. It made her angry all over again when she thought about it. Burnah went out like a bitch and she could never forget what he did.

In her typical attire of sweats and a baby doll tee, Gina sat in her bed with her *Subway* and snacks she got from the *99¢ Store* on La Cienaga Boulevard. The only things she did was go to school and come home. She wouldn't accept anyone's calls and would tell her mother to tell them that she wasn't home. Her jaw was healed, but her arm still had some time before she could get the cast off. That was the main reason she stayed holed up in the house. The stares and inquiries of how she broke her arm annoyed her so much.

Just as she was finishing her food, Serry walked into the room. He did not have a smile on his face. Gina was ignoring him and he didn't like it one bit.

"Why you ignoring my calls, Munchie?" He sat on the leather couch that sat in her room.

"I haven't been wanting to talk. Can you go? I'll call you later," she remarked, dismissively.

"Naw, you got me fucked up. I came to see you, so that's what I'm about to do." Serry insisted, removing his shoes and Oakland Raiders hat.

"Uggghhhhh!" Gina feigned annoyance and rolled her eyes.

The truth was that she was happy to see Serry. She was developing feelings for him, but after dealing with Burnah, she wasn't sure if she should take it there with Serry. Though he was rude as hell, he had a sweet side and Gina loved that about him. She was happy that the streets didn't stress him out or have his ego soaring through the roof, like it did Burnah. Serry was a breath of fresh air and Gallardo didn't seem to mind that he hung around her.

"You might as well cut all that shit out. A nigga about to nap for a little bit and then I gotta hit the streets. Wake me up in like two hours." Serry replied, ignoring the little tantrum she was throwing.

"Unt uhn, you know damn well you are not about to get in my bed with them street clothes on."

"Oh, shit. I forgot." Serry removed his dark blue Levi's shorts and his Oakland Raiders jersey.

He was standing in his boxer briefs, socks and a fresh white wife beater. Gina could see the print of his dick, but she cleared her throat and focused her eyes on the TV. Serry slipped into the bed and two minutes later, she heard light snoring. Gina watched him for a second and joined him because she needed a nap.

€€€€€€€

When Gina woke up, Serry was gone. She yawned and got out of her bed. On the dresser where her TV was perched, there was a jewelry box and a wad of cash sitting on there. Gina picked up the jewelry box and opened it. She gushed over the heart pendant that was inside. It was a beautiful rose gold pendant full of rose colored diamonds.

Just as she was about to text Serry to ask what the occasion was, her bedroom door opened. Kienna walked in with two bags, one on each of her shoulders.

"Good, you're up! We have to get ready."

"Ready for what?" Gina was confused by what she was saying.

"You forgot, didn't you?" Kienna asked, placing the bags on the bed.

"Forgot what?"

"The Rihanna concert is tonight at The Forum. We have to get ready. It starts at seven-thirty."

"Oh, shit! I forgot all about that concert."

"Well, we have a little less than two hours, so get your bighead ass to it and get ready."

"Fuck you, hoe." Gina shot her middle finger up at her best friend.

"Naw, I don't get down like that. Plus, my boo gives me the dick on a regular." Kienna replied, jokingly.

"Uggghhhhh! TMI, hoe!" Gina laughed and rolled her eyes.

"You could be getting dicked down too, if you give my friend a chance." Kienna was referring to Serry.

"Let me go get ready for this concert, so I can see my boo, Rih Rih," Gina changed the subject.

She wasn't ready to address the fact that she wanted to be with him. Serry was everything that Burnah wasn't. She just was afraid to jump into something with him. Every man started off nice and then the lies start stacking up. Gina wasn't trying to go through another heartbreak.

"BITCH BETTER HAVE MY MONEY!" Gina yelled as Rihanna had the whole crowd in pure pandemonium.

They were at the front of the stage. Gina was wearing her pink crop top and skirt set and some knee high boots. She accessorized the outfit with a Future hat, big clear lensed glasses, and the rose gold pendant Serry bought her. Her and Kienna wore matching outfits.

Gina was having so much fun at the concert and this was the most thoughtful gift anyone ever gave her.

No man, besides her brother, cousin, and father had ever taken the time out to consider her feelings or find out the things she enjoyed. When he bought her things for her birthday, Serry didn't realize that his thoughtfulness was what made her like him. She didn't care for the extravagance, but it was a good touch.

After the concert, they decided to ride to Noir and see if the fellas were in there. They drank bottles of Moët and Hennessy on the way. At the stoplight, they noticed a Blue old school Impala on the side of them. They were bumping some old Snoop Dogg. The guy on the passenger side let the window down and he was ugly as hell. He interrupted the ladies' impromptu *SnapChat* party session and signaled for them to let their window down.

"Wassup, ladies! Where y'all headed?" The guy asked them.

The weed smoke made the inside of the car so cloudy that they couldn't see who else in the car, but they could hear them.

"To the club," Kienna replied, dryly.

"Can we roll through wit' y'all? Y'all sexy as fuck?" The guy from the passenger side tried to spit game.

"No, thank you. We have boyfriends." Gina responded, just as the light was changing.

"Fine...I ain't want y'all bitches anyway! Just for that, y'all asses gonna die tonight!" The ugly dude screwed his face up and pulled out a gun and started blasting.

TAT! TATTTTTT! TAT! TAT! POW! POW!

Kienna pressed down on the gas as hard as she could and they raced down the street as bullets whizzed through the truck. They were lucky that none of them had hit them.

Gina pressed the home button, furiously on her phone and Siri's voice came on. Her phone was plugged through the Bluetooth system of Kienna's Aston Martin.

"Call Serry!" She yelled, once Siri asked for what action she wanted to take.

They were on Rosecrants before the bullets stopped and the Impala sped off.

"Ay, wassup, Munch? How was the concert and shit?" Serry answered the phone on the second ring.

"Serry, someone was just shooting at us!" Gina replied, in a shaky voice.

"What the fuck? Where y'all at? Me and Allure about to pull up." Serry yelled out, as she heard him rounding up his crew.

"We are on Rosecrans by the *Jack In The Box*."

"Aight, I'll be there in a few." Serry assured her as he ran to his Maserati.

It belonged to Burnah, but since he was about to be a distant memory, Gallardo gave it to him.

Gina and Kienna got out of the car and waited for Serry and Allure. Both of them were a wreck and scared as hell. They were used to this life, but neither of them had ever been involved in a live shooting. They sat on the curb and could hear sirens in the background. Gina wished that her brother was in town, but she knew that he was in Miami for his birthday.

Serry arrived a few minutes later and Gina ran into his arms.

"Ay, shit going to be straight, ma. I'm sorry ya had to go through that, but them niggas gonna get theirs." Serry spat, mad as hell as he surveyed the damage of the car and how close that Gina could have been to losing her life.

"Don't leave me tonight." Gina whispered, tears still falling from her eyes.

"I won't. Yo' ass coming to the crib wit' me. That ain't up for discussion. Kienna's ass is coming too. Humble's orders."

"Okay."

After being questioned by the cops, Kienna and Gina loaded into Serry's Maserati and they drove to the crib he shared with Humble in Long Beach. They didn't stay too far away from Compton. Gina fell asleep while in the car because she was tired from all of the chaos that took place. Before she went to sleep, she told Serry about how the man looked and the old school car that he was in. She was sure that, that would help them find who shot at them. She was thankful for Serry because Gina wouldn't have been able to calm down without him.

€€€€€€€

She woke up to a dark room that she knew wasn't her own. She looked around and noticed that from the slivers of moonlight, it was Serry's room. He was sitting in his windowsill in all black. She knew that he went out looking for the dudes that shot at her and Kienna. He noticed that she was up when she coughed, her mouth dry from screaming and sleeping.

"You good, Munchie?" He asked, in concern.

"Yes, I'm good. Are you okay?"

"I'm good now. Couldn't find them niggas, but I got some young heads that got their ears to the streets. I'm just glad nothing happened to yo' lil aggy ass." He laughed, to make light of the situation.

"Shut up!" Gina sucked her teeth and smiled at him.

"Come take a shower with me." Serry stood up and placed his gun on the windowsill.

He removed his shirt and made his way to the bathroom. He turned the water on and started stripping. He was down to his boxers when Gina made it to the bathroom. She was butt ass naked and staring at him with a glint of nervousness in her eyes.

Serry licked his lips and stared at her with his eyes slitted, in lust. He pulled his boxers down and beckoned Gina over to him. She sauntered over and jumped in his arms, wrapping her legs around his waist. They engaged in a deep kiss and Serry held her up by her ass.

"Damn, you're beautiful as fuck." He growled, kissing her some more.

"Uhmmm," an involuntary moan escaped from her lips.

Serry carried her to the shower and gently placed her back against the tiled wall. Once she was settled on the wall, he gently entered her honey pot.

"Damn, that pussy juicy and tight." Serry moaned, inserting more inches inside.

"Oooohhhhh!" Gina moaned loudly with her eyes closed.

"It feel good don't it?"

"Yesssss! Damn, it feels soooo good! Serrrryyy!!!"

"I love the way you say my name. Fuckkkk!" Serry yelled out, as they continued to sex one another.

They remained sexing through the night and Gina couldn't believe how good Serry's dick was. She was glad that he was feeling her like she was feeling him. She would just have to talk to Gallardo about this. She didn't want a repeat of what happened between herself and Burnah. Only time would tell if Serry was the one for her or not. She was falling for his savage ass.

"After tonight, yo' lil ass is mine and that's on God." Serry remarked, his voice full of sleep.

"There's no other place I want to be." Gina responded, placing velvety smooth kisses along his chest.

"Keep playing and ya ass gonna wake this dick up," Serry forewarned Gina, with a smile.

"Maybe that's what I want to do." Gina challenged him, with her eyebrows knitted, in curiosity.

"Ride my shit back to life then." Serry grabbed her up and gently placed her opening around the head of his penis.

"We definitely have to talk to my brother and cousin about this." Gina moaned out.

"Shit, I'm doing that tomorrow. Now, shut up and fuck me to sleep." Serry demanded, smacking her on the ass and watching it jiggle in his hands.

29

NEHEMIAH

*N*ehemiah and his crew had been watching Thai's every move since she came back to town. They were waiting on the right time to kidnap her. They were trying to bring the Black Mask Militia to its knees. They couldn't stand them niggas and they wanted them to know that they weren't untouchable out here. Nehemiah's main focus was to hurt Gallardo, so he could get to Nikayla. Nik Nik had always been someone he wanted since he first met her through Nathan. He didn't care that she was his brother's girl. Now that he saw her getting serious with Gallardo, she was becoming an enemy as well. Everyone around them would see that Nehemiah was no one to fuck around with. He was in the midst plotting and scheming on how to mess with the BMM, individually and the women that they loved. The plans he set forth with Mia were working well and he couldn't be any happier.

Both of them were finding enjoyment in doing drugs, having sex, and wreaking havoc. Before it was all said and done, they were going to make some blood shed from somebody, if not the whole crew. They were not untouchable and Nehemiah felt like in reality, they were weak as fuck. Driven by nothing, but jealousy and greed. Nehemiah planned to take over their traps and the territory around it. It would not only be a win-win for him, but his crew as well. He felt like they were nickel and diming, but this takeover would guarantee that their pockets would be stacked.

"There that hoe go right there!" Crazy Carl pointed out, as he took a hit of the cocaine-laced joint in his mouth.

"Y'all ready to do this shit?" Nehemiah asked his niggas.

"Hell yeah," they all answered, in unison.

"Masks on. Let's get this shit over with." Nehemiah and the men slipped on their face shields and moved in the shadows of the night.

Thai lived on Slauson Ave. in Blood gang territory, so they had to be swift and snatch her up. They couldn't chance being caught up in this neighborhood. All of them would be dead. When they saw that the coast was clear, they walked to the back of the apartments and broke the streetlights, so they could remain as clandestine as possible. The darkness would be their advantage. They all lied I wait on Thai's back porch, so that they could break in and snatch her out of the house. Nehemiah was nervous, but he wouldn't let that show. This plan had to come together without a hitch and fear would just have them making mistakes that they couldn't afford to make.

*T*hai was back from New Jersey and they were trying to make an effort to be cordial since she was pregnant with KB's seed. He was excited to be having his first child. It was the first time ever that he was thinking about leaving the game and feeling a woman on a level other than her swallowing his kids after they were done. He didn't ever shoot up the club, so in his eyes, Thai had to be special. He just couldn't put his finger on it.

Since she still wasn't talking to him, he decided he was going to break in her crib like he usually did. He arrived on her block and killed his engine. He noticed that the street and the lights around the apartments were broken out, but it didn't alarm him.

He figured that the hustling niggas knocked them out like they did whenever they was up to no good. Taking the gun from his glove compartment, he placed it into the small of his back and headed to the back where Thai's apartment was located. KB knew that she was in the house because the truck he gave her was parked outside. As he was heading to the stairs, he noticed five figures in all black crouched down on Thai's back porch. Pulling his gun out, he started busting his bullets at them.

"Y'all fuck niggas done lost y'all minds fucking with my bitch!" KB voice boomed.

The sound of the bullets from his gun and the impact they were making could be heard throughout the apartments. The men scrambled to get away from KB's aim. He ran after the ones who jumped from the banister to get away. One of them laid dead on the back porch and one was sliding against the pavement, to safety. The rest of them managed to get away as KB ran down the block blasting his gun. He didn't stop until he heard the clicking sound, letting him know that he ran out of bullets. Heading to his car, he pressed the button to the secret compartment in his armrest. That was where he kept the rest of his guns. Pulling one out, he closed the compartment back and ran over to the wounded man in the middle of the road.

"Who the fuck sent you, nigga?" KB asked, as he aimed his gun at the man.

It appeared that he was shot in the torso and leg. He was crying and still trying to slide to the curb.

"Fuck you! You...need...to...know this shit ain't over!" The man spoke and then spit a blob of bloody saliva into KB's face.

"Wrong answer, bitch nigga!" KB sent two bullets into his head, silencing him for good.

Reaching into his pocket, KB pulled out his cellphone and called Gallardo. After getting off the phone with him, he ran to the back of Thai's apartment and let himself in.

"THAI!" He yelled out, to get her attention.

"In the back," she yelled, in a shaky voice.

"Pack some shit! We gotta get the fuck out of here. I just had to body two niggas! They was trying to break in here."

"What?" Thailand was dumbfounded by this happening.

"Yeah, we may have to go to Jersey and cool off. Until then, you coming to the crib with me." KB called out, as he helped her pack her stuff up.

This wasn't how the night was planned for KB, but nothing was ever typical when it came to being a member of the *Black Mask Militia*. Gallardo arrived and told them to leave and that he had things from there. KB wanted to protest, but he knew that Gallardo wasn't one to play with when he had to repeat himself. KB and Thailand hopped in their cars and headed to his crib. They would discuss things when they got there. KB said a silent prayer and hoped that things would get better for the crew. It seemed like every time they · turned around some shit was happening.

HEAVY

*H*eavy sat in the cold interrogation room, waiting for someone to come inside of there. When KB called him and told him that he had to murk some mark ass nigga for trying to kidnap Thai, he pulled up and told them to leave. One time pulled up and took him in for questioning. They had him in this room as if they wanted him to confess or something. He kept his composure and waited to see what kind of shenanigans that they planned to pull. Gallardo was no stranger to the law. He was used to them sniffing around and he knew they were gunning for him after the whole Doon situation. Doon was still missing and so were the papers from the affidavit as well. He hoped that they hurried up. He hated the stale décor and sterile smell of police stations. It was a place that made him uncomfortable to be. It wasn't something he could get used to.

Finally, two detectives walked in and Gallardo rolled his eyes, upward. By the way that they walked in, it looked like they were about to play the good detective, bad detective game. He wasn't even surprised. One time tried to pull anything out their ass to get you to confess. They didn't care if you did it or not. Their goal was to bait you and separate the weak from the strong.

The detectives sat down and sure enough, they were about to play that game. It took everything for Gallardo not to laugh in their faces. One detective, a tall Latino man was sitting there in silence, with a screw face, while the other one, a short, black detective had a smile on his face. He was probably sent in to "relate" to him. Y'all mother-fuckers need to step y'all game up. Everybody ain't falling for this dumb shit. Gallardo mused to himself.

The black detective started to speak.

"Good evening, Gallardo. Sorry, we kept you waiting. We had some other things that required our dire attention. How are you feeling? I'm Detective Adams and this is Detective Sanchez." He tried to appeal to him with that nice role.

"Can y'all cut to the chase. This good cop, bad cop shit is played out, bruh."

"Your black ass got a smart mouth I see," the Latino detective spat, mugging Gallardo.

"My mama used to tell me the same thing, growing up."

"Oh, imma enjoy this. Since you want to be such a smart ass, I'm going to keep you down here for the rest of the night, motherfucker!" Detective Sanchez looked like he wanted break Gallardo in two.

Gallardo was waiting because he was going to sue the hell out of the LAPD. They were known for getting physical, so he would win his case.

"Look, Mr. Miller, we could easily charge you with the murder of those two guys, but I have a feeling you didn't do that. I'm sure you can point me in the direction of who did. Can't you?" Detective Adams was now speaking again and trying to reel in a confession or to get him to snitch.

Either way, it wasn't happening. They had nothing on him.

"I don't know anything about that. I was coming to check on my homegirl at her house and she wasn't home. All that other stuff you talking is irrelevant.

"I'm going to enjoy locking your black ass up for this." The Latino one, chuckled angrily.

Before Gallardo could say anything else, the door opened. They all looked up to see who was entering the room. It was the family lawyer, Arthur Prescott and his recruiter, Chief Smith. Gallardo was happy to see both of them and knew that he was okay now.

"Unless you're formally charging my client, I suggest that you let him go." Prescott called out to the detectives.

"I'm going to charge him with suspicion of murder!" Detective Sanchez yelled, indignantly as he beat his hands against the table.

"My client has already told you that he was not involved with the death of those two gentlemen. You did not find any weapons or anything to question him about."

"He can go now. Mr. Miller, we will be in touch." Detective Adams looked over at him.

"Indeed." Gallardo gave them a smile and stood up from the chair he was sitting in.

The three men exited the interrogation room and Gallardo went to go pick up his belongings. Once he signed out, all three of them left the police building and headed to the parking lot.

"Thank you, man for being there for me, Chief." Gallardo thanked his recruiter.

"No thanks needed. Just keep your nose clean until you head out of here to Illinois."

"Will do, sir." Gallardo shook Chief Smith's hand and they went their separate ways.

His lawyer had already left once he received his retainer. Gallardo grabbed his phone and called an Uber. He needed to make it to the trap house on Westmont. Sending out a mass text message to the crew, he drove to his destination with a lot on his mind. This encounter with LAPD was another close call and he needed to get out of the streets before anything else happened. His freedom was hanging in the balance.

Arriving at the trap house, he saw that his crew beat him there. He was glad for that. That way he didn't have to say what he was about to say, more than once. Killing his engine, Gallardo walked up to the porch and let himself in the door. Zip, Humble, Tress, Allure, and Serry sat at the card table in the room, waiting for him. KB wasn't coming to the meeting because Gallardo wanted him to lay low and be there for Thailand.

After dapping everyone up, Gallardo took a seat at the table with his crew.

"I know y'all probably wondering why I called y'all here...well, this is not a social call, my niggas."

"Yo, cuz, you good?" Zip looked over to him.

"Yeah, I'm good. I just need y'all to figure out that exit strategy y'all gonna take."

"Exit strategy? What you mean?" Serry asked, confusingly.

"The Feds have us in their radar and it's best that we lay low for a while. Zip and I are handing things over to Humble. I'm out." Gallardo replied, matter-of-factly.

"Yo, you serious?" Allure inquired, somewhat dumbfounded.

"Yep."

"All of y'all need to think of something. This shit ain't promised and it look like niggas are trying to come after us and all. G taking his ass to the Navy, but I still will be here. We just gonna continue to do shit like we are doing, but move smart. Y'all get it?"

Every man in the room shook their heads, in agreement. They spoke on more Black Mask Militia business and then Gallardo dismisses everyone.

"This meeting is adjourned. Aight, Keep them eyes open because them niggas plotting. Have the banga on ya to show em the militia behind ya."

"Same shit, different day, when the militia is behind ya," the men responded, simultaneously.

He had Humble stay behind, so he could talk to him about the changes that were going to be made. There was a lot of ground to cover, in so little time. He hoped that things went well because he felt that Humble was the perfect candidate to take over.

*T*hings with Suri was going so well that Zip made sure he wasn't on any drama or bullshit. He was enjoying her company and she was good with Zasaya. Since Zasaya was staying with him on a regular basis, Suri volunteered to watch her when he was running the streets. She was always a good girl, but now he was seeing that he made a fucked up decision choosing Saya back in the day. She was proving to be the baby mama from hell. She was neglecting her seed and it was a rumor going around that she was fucking with crack. Zip hadn't caught her in the act, but the source who told him was reliable as fuck. Wasn't anybody in the *Black Mask Militia* selling to her, so he knew she was probably getting the shit from East Compton, in Crip territory. Them niggas didn't care who they sold that shit to. It pissed him off to know that his ex was a basehead. He had a reputation in these streets and even though they weren't together, a nigga would try her just because she was his baby mama. Saya wasn't built for this street shit, so a nigga would get her strung out and try to use it against him.

Zip, Zasaya, and Suri had just come from her soccer game. He had a lot of more free time, since they were slowing down in the game. Since all of the crazy shit that they had been experienced, himself and Gallardo thought it was best for them to chill for a little while. Their traps were getting robbed, niggas were coming up dead, Gina and Kienna got shot at, at the Rihanna concert, KB's girl almost got kidnapped and they were under the Feds' radar for some reason. Every morning, Zip saw a black sedan parked outside of his house. The shit was nerve wracking and they had to figure out something before all of them ended up in prison. Zip had been really leaning toward going legit and just working at the mechanic shop full time. It was a different tune from him saying the streets had a hold on him. If he continued to be out there, the Feds were going to make sure that he was under the jail.

As he drove them back to his house in Long Beach, Zip was really trying to figure out this exit strategy in his head. After the meeting with Gallardo, this may be the best time to leave the game. He gave them the option of laying low and regrouping, but with him having Zasaya full time and this thing with Suri heating up, he may have to re-evaluate his life.

"Babe, you good?" Suri asked him, as she saw the look of angst on his face.

"Yeah, a nigga is straight. Just was thinking about some shit." Zip assures her, turning the corner to his block.

"I'm here if you need to talk." She looked him into the eyes, so he knew she was being sincere.

"I know." Zip kissed her hand and focused back on the road.

As he pulled into his driveway, he instantly recognized Saya as she stood off to the side of his house. His anger rose as he took in her appearance. The rumors were true. She was on crack because Saya looked like a shell of herself. Her hair was unkempt and all over her head, she had lost a dramatic amount of weight that the clothes she was hanging off of her. Zasaya was asleep, so didn't see her mother like this. Zip didn't want something like this to be seared in her memory. He got out of his truck and went to the backseat to pull Zasaya out. He passed the keys to Suri and they headed to his door, so she could open.

"Keep yo' ass right here!" Zip demanded, gruffly to Saya.

He went to go take his daughter uspstairs to her room. He couldn't believe that Saya had some nerve to show up to his house looking the way that she did. When he made it back upstairs, her and Suri were arguing in each other's faces. Zip moved Suri out of the way and told her to go in the house. Listening to what he said, Suri rolled her eyes and slammed the door behind her.

"Why the fuck are you here, Saya?" Zip folded his arms across his chest.

"I came to see my baby. Saya spoke, hoping it would convince him.

"Bitch, are you serious right now? Get off of my porch, Saya before I break yo' fucking neck!" He raised his voice and could see the fear in her eyes.

"Yes, I'm serious! You can't keep me away from my child!" She called herself getting back loud with him.

"News flash, hoe...I didn't keep you away from your child, yo' ass disappeared on some dumb shit!"

"I had to take care of some things. I'm back now."

"Really, bitch?" Zip laughed, but there wasn't a damn thing funny. "Yo, Saya, get the fuck off my porch."

"So, you really going to have that bitch around my daughter. You know I don't like her." Saya rolled her neck and acted like she had any say so in what Zip chose to do with his life.

"Chill on my girl. She been here...that's more than I say for yo' unfit ass."

"I will take yo' ass to court, Zacarion! Don't make me do it!" Saya threatened, knowing that Zip hated all forms of law enforcement and the judicial system, as a whole.

"Bitch please! I'm warning you to get the fuck on!" Zip grimaced, getting pissed off.

"What are you going to do? Hit me?" Saya chortled like it was the funnest thing in the world to think of.

"I won't hit a woman, but guaranteed a bitch can get Super Saiyan punched with no remorse. You got ten seconds to get the fuck out of my sight with your burnt out ass. I should fill your snorting ass with lead right now. Stay the fuck away from my daughter or you will really see why they call me, Zip! Fuck off my porch, you leaving crack and bum bitch residue. Fucking sack chaser !" Zip growled out and slammed the door in her face.

"I can't believe this funky bitch—," He was interrupted during his rant.

"Zacarion, I came back to LA to be closer to my mom. Yeah, I was fucked up when you got Saya pregnant, but I'm over it. Fuck her, but if she ever roll up on me again in life, your child won't have a mother." Suri pointed out, no remnants of a smile on her face, so he knew that she was serious.

"Aight, gangsta, do what you gotta do. For now, imma need you to bust that pussy open for me." Zip let her know just what he wanted, knowing that it would help her get out of her feelings.

"Oh, yeah. What you going to do for me?" She asked, curious to know how this would benefit her as well.

She knew, but she wanted him to say it.

"Imma fuck the shit out of you and eat the fuck out of you too. " Zip picked her up over his shoulder and ran upstairs, so they could participate in a little bedroom play.

€€€€€€€

A few days later...

Zip sat inside of Noir drinking and having a good time. He was stressed from all of the extra work he was putting in to get out of the game. Since Gallardo was about to pursue a career in the Navy, everything fell back on Zip. He was in charge of all things Black Mask Militia until Humble was competent enough to take over. They all had just returned from Columbia to run things by Enrikqto, so he knew of the changes that were about to take forth. The only people that were unhappy with the changes were Zip and Gallardo's fathers. They felt like Zip and Gallardo were giving up too soon and the business should stay in the family. They didn't care because the Feds was not something either of them wanted to get involved with. Once

Humble took over, they all would lay low for a while and then business would be back like it never left.

Zip took a sip of the Grey Goose and passionfruit juice he ordered from the bar and vibed to the music. He was three drinks in and was feeling a little buzz. The new bartender, Tasha was making him think about bending her over. She was a pretty woman and she smelled great. Zip was the only one in the VIP section and she was only serving him. He stared at her ass, while it swayed from left to right. The shit was huge and seemed to have a mind of its own.

"Would you like anything else to drink, Mr. Miller?" Tasha addressed him, as she stood to wait to see what he would say.

"Another Goose and Passionfruit." Zip called out, as he swished the ice that was in the empty cup in his hand.

"Coming right up." She winked at him and smiled.

Zip could feel himself giving in to temptation and had to put a stop to it. Suri was a good girl and he wanted to continue to do right by her. When he tried to get up from the velvet couch in the section, his head started spinning. He had to take a seat to alleviate the woozy feeling in his body. Zip's eyes were getting heavy and he knew he was probably past his limit. He could hear the loud music blaring around him, but he was stuck in place.

€€€€€€€

"Shitttttttt!" Zip groaned out, as he felt the sensations from someone bobbling their face down on his dick.

It was pitch black in the room, so he didn't know who it was or where he was. All Zip remembered was almost losing his footing when he stood in the club. Everything else was foggy.

Suri has yet to give him head, so he thought she was being spontaneous and finally blessing him with her throat action. He used his hand and guided her head along his shaft. He was still in a drunken haze, so the sounds and slipperiness of this head had his mind gone.

"Fuck!" Zip yelled out, in pleasure.

He didn't even know that his life was in danger. Tasha was really

Mia and she was preparing to call Nehemiah, so they could kill him. This was all a part of their plan, just like all of the other things that were happening to the crew.

As she continued to suck his dick, they heard banging on the door. Zip's senses heightened as the knocking got louder and louder. He didn't have his gun on his hip, when he felt to see.

KNOCK! KNOCK! BOOM! BOOM!

"ZACARION, OPEN THIS FUCKING DOOR! I KNOW YOUR ASS IN THERE! OPEN IT NOW OR IMMA BREAK THIS MOTH-ERFUCKER OFF THE HINGES!" He heard Suri's voice and it was laced in pure rage.

He was confused because he could have sworn that this was Suri giving him this A1 blowjob. Zip jumped up and reached for the light. When he looked over at the bed, it was "Tasha" sitting there, with a smile on her face.

His gun laid on the nightstand. Looking at the nightstand drawer, he saw that they were in The W Los Angeles. Zip was confused on how they got there and wondering how the hell he was going to get out of this.

"FUCKKKK!" He kicked the bed, in frustration.

"Who is that?" Tasha asked, faking like she was scared.

"My girl," Zip announced, pulling his pants up and fixing his belt.

"Ohmigod! I'm sorry about this. I didn't know."

"It's cool. This shit on me, ma." Zip let out a sigh of defeat.

He went to the door and unlocked it. Suri burst through the door, with her sister, Morgan right behind her. She stared at the rumpled bedsheets and a half-naked Tasha. She stood there for a second and started attacking Zip.

"Just when I decided to take a chance on you, your dog ass in the hotel with some bitch! How could you do this to me?"

"Man, baby, I don't even remember how I got here." Zip held on to his head because he had a headache and still was confused on how he got here.

"See, I would've believed your lying ass, had you not butt dialed me and I heard you telling this bitch she had good pussy and so on.

To think I was falling for you! FUCK YOU!" She yelled, through tears.

"Suri Uri, I really don't know what's going on!"

"Goodbye, Zacarion!" Suri yelled and stole off on "Tasha" one good time.

She exited the room with Morgan and Zip just stood there, his mind scrambling to figure out what was going on. All he knew is that he had to try to get Suri back. She was his world, next to his daughter. How could I be so motherfucking stupid? He scolded himself. Without any more thought, he grabbed his cellphone and keys and ran out of the hotel door to chase her. All he knew was that he couldn't let her leave his life again.

33

GG

*T*hree months later...

"So, what does it say?" Nikayla asked Gretchen, as she walked out of the bathroom.

Her expression was hard to read, so Nikayla couldn't gauge an expression from it.

"You are definitely pregnant, love." Gretchen revealed to Nikayla, with a smile.

"Ayyyyeee, I'm so happy about this. I just wish that Gallardo could hear the news right now." Nikayla responded, sadly.

Gallardo was in Illinois for basic training, so he wasn't able to know about the news just yet.

"I'm sure my brother will be very happy when he does find out." GG was trying to calm her down.

"I'm sure that you are right. I love him very much." Nikayla smiled and confessed.

" I can see it in your eyes. I haven't seen you happy like this in a while. I love it." Gretchen gushed, as she hugged her best friend.

"I'm truly in a happy place. I have you to thank for that though. Thank you so much for being my best friend and always being there for me, Gretchen. It means the world to me." Nikayla smiled as she expressed her feelings to GG.

They continued to talk and eat the food they bought from Loreto's Fried Turkey and Louisiana Fried Chicken.

When GG finished hanging with Nikayla, she headed to her internship with *BASE Architecture, Planning & Engineering Inc.* It was an African American architectural firm located in Venice. She was in her last two semesters in school, so she spent most of her time there. UCLA's master program requires an internship after the undergraduate level, as well. She enjoyed working there and was gaining valuable experience. She planned to go into business with Tress once she finished school.

Arriving at BASE, Gretchen walked into the building and spoke to the security guard, Teisha. Teisha was raised in Compton, So GG knew her from around the way.

"Hey, boo!"

"Wassup, girl! I didn't even think that you was coming in today."

"Oh, yeah...I asked Mr. Davis to give me some time to finish this assignment I had for class."

"You keep doing your thing, love. I'm about to catch the elevator with you since my relief is here to take over down here."

"Okay, cool." GG and Teisha stepped on the elevator and rode it to the tenth floor.

When the elevator door opened, Gretchen saw Tress standing by the receptionist's desk. She walked over to see what he wanted.

"Hey, babe. Have you been here long?"

"Naw, I had a meeting that I gotta talk to you about later. I just got here a few minutes ago." Tress let it be known and she let out a sigh of relief.

"I went over to see Nik Nik to cheer her up a little. She is a little down that Gallardo's gone."

"Yeah, I went over there yesterday and took her, Naheem, and Khaleem to get some dinner and stuff."

"Well, I don't have an office, but there is an office area for me and the other two interns. We can go in there."

"Naw, I gotta get out of here soon and just wanted to run something by you."

By then, Gretchen's attention was in the pile of assignments Mr. Davis gave her for the day.

"What is it?" She finally looked at him and her breath got caught in her throat.

Tress was kneeled down on one knee and looking up at her. The tears started falling as she stared at Tress.

"I don't have a long and crazy speech written out. I've been thinking about this for a long time. All I know is that I want you in my life forever. Please make me the luckiest man ever...Gretchen Serita Miller, will you be my wife?"

"Yes, Tresshaun Alexander Stephens, I'll marry you." Tress got up from his knee and kissed her.

There was a boisterous eruption of applause around them. They were only focused on each other. Gretchen was so happy in this moment. She had an announcement of her own. She planned to tell Tress later. This moment was so lovely. She was happy that things were coming together for them.

34

NIKAYLA

*N*ikayla was a nervous wreck as she got herself together. Gallardo was graduating from basic training, so everyone was taking a plane to be there for him. She missed him, so much and couldn't wait until he saw her belly. She was five months pregnant and carried her pregnancy very well. Everyone doted over her. Gretchen and Tress were the only ones who knew the sex of the baby and she wanted them to reveal it to Gallardo at the graduation.

Since he left, Naheem and Khaleem stepped up like they were the men of the house. She thought it was cute and felt spoiled. They made sure that on Nikayla's down days that they didn't run her crazy and took care of her every whim. Since Khaleem could drive, he took care of her crazy cravings. She was thankful for her boys. They came through when she needed them.

They sat in the auditorium of *Naval Station Great Lakes* in Chicago. There were over five hundred men graduating, so they had to wait a while to hear Gallardo's name being called. All of them jumped up and yelled for him. They all were proud to see him walk across that stage.

Once the ceremony was over, Gallardo walked over to Nikayla

and picked her up. It was an emotional moment for them. He wiped her tears away and kissed her on the lips.

"Damn, I've been wanting to do this for months now," Gallardo smiled and then looked down at her stomach. "Wowwww! You got me so happy right now!"

"I'm eight months now." Nikayla let him know.

"Ayyyyeee! That's wassup."

Gallardo greeted the rest of his family and they all went to the mess hall for the refreshments and food they had in there.

For a few more hours, Gallardo enlightened them on the journey it took for him to become an U.S. Navy sailor. The men filled him in on what was going on in the streets. Nikayla could tell that he missed his old life.

Finally having Nikayla alone, he grabbed her up and placed her in his lap.

"We are about to go to Puerto Rico. I need some alone time with you because a nigga backed up." Gallardo whispered in her ear and nibbled on it.

"Ooohhh, really?" Nikayla was excited to be going to Puerto Rico.

She had always wanted to go there and Gallardo knew that. He made it possible and she couldn't be any happier.

"I don't have anything packed." Nikayla tried to explain to him.

"Me either. We can buy all of that shit in PR. Just focus on me fucking the shit out of your fine ass."

"Okay." They kissed again and everyone started clowning them.

"Y'all need to get a room with all that lovey dovey shit." Serry blurted out, causing everyone to laugh and Gallardo's mother to slap him in the back of his head.

"Don't hate on me because my girl love me with your ugly ass!" Gallardo replied back to Serry.

"I know one thing, y'all better stop all that damn cursing around me." His mother scolded them.

"Sorry, mama." Gallardo apologized and grabbed Nikayla's hand, so he could help her up.

They said their goodbyes to the family and went outside to catch an Uber to *O'Hare International Airport.* Nikayla was so happy to be getting away with the love of her life. They had been apart for three months and now they were in each other's presence.

They both slept the whole time that they were on the plane. Gallardo definitely took advantage of these few hours of slumber because he hadn't slept much while he was in basic training. Nikayla was tired from the baby in her belly.

€€€€€€€€

It took four hours for them to get to Puerto Rico and they both were hyped. They took in the pure blue waters, lush vegetation, and the beautiful flowers spread around the island. This place was breathtaking in every way. Even the projects had them entranced. Their guide, Hector was showing them all around San Juan. Gallardo arranged for them to see the sights and then head to the mall to shop for the things they would need during this two-day trip. After this trip, Gallardo would have to leave for another month for training related to his career.

The Mall of San Juan was huge. They had all kinds of stores that reminded them of California. Gallardo walked through store after store with Nikayla as she browsed through items and chose the ones she wanted. He didn't mind spending time or money on his girl. It was his duty to provide for her and their children. There was so many bags that Hector and Gallardo made three trips to the Mercedes-Benz G-Wagon. Gallardo paid him handsomely to drive them around town and let him pick out some things he would like.

"Babe, I'm loving it here already. Puerto Rico is so beautiful." Nikayla gushed, as they sat in *BRIO Tuscan Grille* enjoying a light dinner.

All of that shopping made them work up an appetite.

"Yeah, it is dope as hell here. I can see myself coming back. Next time, we gotta bring Khaleem and Naheem. How have they been?"

"They have been great. Helping me sail through this pregnancy."

"That's great to hear. I hate that I wasn't there for you during that time."

"It's fine, babe. I didn't even know I was five months pregnant until the OB/GYN told me at my first appointment." Nikayla explained to him, trying to ease his mind.

"I still should've been there. All I was thinking about was getting the hell out of dodge before the Feds tried to build a case on me."

"I understand why you had to leave and I'm okay with it, my love. You had to do what you had to do."

"Just as late mg as you know I wasn't on no selfish shit, we good." Gallardo replied, staring at her, intensely.

"Can we head to the hotel now. I'm ready to ride the hell out of you, right now."

"Let me pay this check and we can go."

After a great session of love making, both of them were covering in sweat and just basking in the aftermath of it all. It got hot and heavy out on the balcony. They were sure that people heard them. They didn't care because they were making up for lost time. Gallardo finished the session by licking and sucking on Nikayla's pussy like it was his last meal. He wanted her to feel how much he missed her by giving her great, AI head.

He noticed Nikayla was trying to doze off, so he nudged her to get her attention. When she looked up at him, he knew that what he had wanted to do for the longest, was inevitable. She searched his eyes and noticed he was tearing up a little.

"Babe, are you okay?" She was concerned right now because she had never seen him cry before.

"Yeah...I'm good. Just had something on my mind."

"Whatever it is, you can tell me. We are in this together."

"I'm glad you said that because this makes what I want to do, a lot easier."

"Okay, what's going on...you're kind of speaking in riddles, Gallardo."

"I DIDN'T BRING you here just to celebrate me being home from basic training...I brought you here because I can't breathe another gust of air without you being Mrs. Miller. Fuck how soft this make me look right now. I could give a motherfuck. So, you gonna ride for a nigga? A king can't reign without his queen." Gallardo replied, with his head still lying between Nikayla's legs. He had just gave her some mind blowing head. They were sitting on the balcony of their hotel room, overlooking the city of San Juan.

"NIGGA, you just proposed with your tongue inches from my pussy after snatching my soul...where is my ring?" Nikayla exclaimed, truly happy at that moment.

"Hold up." Gallardo hopped out the bed, dick swinging, to retrieve the engagement ring for her.

He rehearsed many times about how he was going to propose to Nikayla, but this moment just seemed right. Yeah, it wasn't the conventional way to ask a woman to marry you, but who the fuck cares. This was their shit and anyone who had something to say about it could mind their business.

Gallardo opened the box and placed the twelve-carat princess-cut, ring dropping with enough diamonds to blind a motherfucker. Nikayla gazed at the ring with a smile. She planted kisses all over his face.

"Okay, now you gotta get up. Your dream wedding awaits." Gallardo smiled at her, sneakily.

Nikayla dijdnt know what he had up under his sleeve, but she wasn't going to question it either. She trusted that Gallardo was the man that she was destined to spend the rest of her life with. Hell, she would marry him in the middle of the streets in Inglewood. The fact that he went out of his way to get her to Puerto Rico, spoke volumes.

The rest of the trip went by well. They made love all over their hotel room, took in more sights, and ate all kinds of foods. They also made plans to go back there. It was too beautiful for them not to come back.

about some graduation party Heavy was throwing at his house. They hadn't seen him in a while and he finally emerged.

As they made it to Heavy's block, all you could hear was the music blasting from the house and the faint sound of several guns cocking. They weren't playing any music in the car. All of them were high from coke and weed. Crazy Carl pressed the gas and the van sped up a little. They noticed Heavy standing outside alone and started busting their guns as the van whirred past him. Seeing his body hit the ground brought satisfaction to the men. They heard someone shooting at them, but they were long gone before it could do any harm.

"Mission accomplished." Nehemiah let out a deep, maniacal laugh that almost made him sound animalistic.

The rest of the men in the car laughed and they headed off into the wind.

EPILOGUE

HEAVY

*P*lanning this party and seeing the smiles on his sister and wife's faces, made Gallardo feel whole. Gretchen and Mikayla both graduated with their Masters from *UCLA*. That was an accomplishment all in itself. With plenty of poking and prodding from his wife and mother, Gallardo went into the Navy Reserves and started going to *Compton Community College* and decided to major in Engineering. It was a great fit because he was great at math and deeply interested in science. He was in his first semester of college and loving it. Though his dad didn't agree with his decision to pass the Black Heart Militia down to Humble, he still did it anyway. After all of the chaos that the crew went through, they all came to the decision that the street life was basically over for them. It was a tough consensus, but it needed to be made for the safety of their families and loved ones.

In the past few months, they all had made several strives in life. Gallardo and Nikayla were expecting a baby boy, any day now, got married in Puerto Rico, and officially adopted Khaleem, even though he was sixteen. They wanted to make him a part of their family. He was a smart and bright kid and Gallardo wanted to make sure that was able to have something in his will, in case something happened to him; Zip and Suri were not together, but both were co-parenting Zasaya. Since she didn't much of a mother, Suri stepped up to help take care of her. Everyone was pissed at Zip for ruining that, but he kept telling them that it wasn't their motherfucking business.

Though Gallardo was against it at first, Serry and his sister, Gina were going stronger and ever. After all of the shit with Burnah, he was leery about his sister dating, especially someone in his crew. Serry proved himself, so Gallardo had to accept it. Everyone else thought they were a great fit. Gina was finishing up her studies at UCLA and managing Gallardo's club, Noir; Tress and Gretchen were engaged and planned on getting married around Christmastime; KB moved to New Jersey with Thai, so she could be closer to her family. She got pregnant the night that they had sex at the hospital, so they had a three-month old daughter named, Kashmira. After she almost got kidnapped, KB thought it would be better for her to be home. Everyone in the crew had their own lives, but the Militia still lived in them all. They were all in attendance for the graduation party and having a great time.

Gallardo stood behind his pregnant wife and kissed her exposed shoulder and neck.

"I love you." He whispered into her ear and nibbled on it.

"I love you, too," she said, loud enough for only him to hear it.

"I'll be right back. I have to go to the car and get you and GG's other gifts." Gallardo moved from behind her and headed out of the gate of Zip's house, so that he could go in his car. Humble ran behind him and tried to get his attention.

"Ay, big homie!" Humble called out, as he ran up to Gallardo.

"Wassup, bruh?"

"I just wanted to get you alone and thank you again for having faith in me to take over the Militia. I'm young as shit, but I promise you I won't let you down." Humble confided to him.

"I know that. When all of us chose to step down, wasn't anybody else I would consider for the job. Just be careful out there and focus on coming back in one piece for your girl."

_na, bruh." They dapped each other up and Humble went in the gate to rejoin the party.

Gallardo headed out of the gate and pressed the alarm on his key fob. The doors unlocked and he went into the trunk to retrieve the two boxes. As he was hunched over in the back, he heard a car moving at a rapid pace down the street. He reached in the back of his waistband and pulled out his trusty .45. Gallardo cocked the gun and stood up. Before he could even shoot, his body was riddled with bullets and his body hit the ground. He had blood gushing from the holes in his body. His breath was rugged. He could hear all of the chaos of his family screaming and the sound of guns blazing around him.

Humble was the first one out of the gate. He started running down the street like a mad man, with his twin Desert Eagles in his hands.

Through the slits of his eyes, he could see Zip holding on to him and tears leaking from his eyes.

"Why. You. Crying. Nigga?" Gallardo managed to get out, in between him catching his breath and spitting up globs of blood.

"Shut up, fool. Keep holding on! Help is coming." Zip tried his best to keep him from closing his eyes.

"Take care of my wife...Naheem...Khaleem...and name my son, Compton...tell him...tell him..." Before Gallardo could finish his sentence, his body started twitching and his eyes were rolling into the back of his.

Zip started crying like a baby as he closed his Gallardo's eyes that were open and still. He died right in there in the driveway. He would never meet his son or enjoy life with Nikayla again. Sometimes the king had to die. This wasn't the happy ending you would assume, but life didn't always work like that. Not exactly like David and Goliath because the beast won this time.

CPSIA information can be obtained
at www.ICGtesting.com
Printed in the USA
LVHW03s1128140818
586845LV00028BA/997/P